Sabine Baring-Gould

The Gaverocks - A Tale of the Cornish Coast

Vol. III

Sabine Baring-Gould

The Gaverocks - A Tale of the Cornish Coast
Vol. III

ISBN/EAN: 9783337082581

Printed in Europe, USA, Canada, Australia, Japan

Cover: Foto ©Andreas Hilbeck / pixelio.de

More available books at **www.hansebooks.com**

THE GAVEROCKS

A TALE OF THE CORNISH COAST

BY THE

AUTHOR OF 'JOHN HERRING' 'MEHALAH' &c.

IN THREE VOLUMES

VOL. III.

LONDON

SMITH, ELDER, & CO., 15 WATERLOO PLACE

1887

CONTENTS

OF

THE THIRD VOLUME.

———◇◇———

THE GAVEROCKS.

CHAPTER XLII.

THE departure of Loveday from Marsland was not so easily managed as Constantine supposed. Days passed without an answer from the Exeter cousin, and at last Loveday's letter was returned from the Dead Letter Office: 'Left Exeter; address not known.'

Loveday was troubled. What should she do? Whither could she go? She must consult Constantine. There was no one else whom she could consult. She was uneasy, anxious to leave, partly because her brother and friends at Towan knew nothing about her —where she was, what she was doing—and also because a continued residence at Marsland was unendurable to her.

She had seen little of Constantine since the interview in the parlour. He had, or pretended to have, business at Stanbury which occupied him so continuously that he slept there, coming to Marsland only now and then.

One beautiful day the opportunity she desired arrived. She was in the garden, sitting on the bench, holding the baby on her lap, talking and singing to it. She was much improved in health, but still looked delicate, and the expression of intense sadness would not wear out of her face, but it was qualified and sweetened by resignation. She had no hope in life, no object towards which she could strive. Sometimes, when she was in the garden with the child, Paul was also there, working, or collecting herbs, and he would talk to her. His conversation always brought her comfort. Without knowing her secret he divined the depth of her trouble, and sympathised with her.

Paul's conversation acted on her hot and suffering heart like the flow over it of cool spring-water.

The child exercised a healing influence also. It drew her attention from herself. She became very fond of it, and it was a pleasure to her to be able to carry it about and amuse it whilst the mother was engaged on her duties in the house. When Loveday was not nursing little Con she was engaged on needlework, repairs which had been neglected after the birth of the child, because Juliot had not time to attend to both.

She had made a little posy of bachelor's-buttons for the baby when the garden door opened, and Constantine came to her. He looked sharply about, to make sure that Paul Featherstone was not there, and then he seated himself on the bench beside Loveday. At the back grew an elder, now a mass of sweetness and white bloom.

'I am glad to find you alone,' said Constantine. 'Why are you still here?'

She told him the reason. He was perplexed, and bit his thumb.

'I thought your cousin was living beyond her income. How is it you did not know this before leaving Nantsillan?'

'I wrote, but left before the return of the letter. It will have arrived, and alarmed my brother : he will not know where I am.'

'There is no help for it,' said Constantine. 'You must remain here a little longer, till something is heard of. I will put an advertisement for you in an Exeter paper. Tell me, have Paul Featherstone and Juliot questioned you regarding the cause of your illness?'

'Oh, Constantine! no. They have vastly too good feeling to do such a thing. But Mr. Featherstone is so wonderful that I fancy at times he sees into my soul and reads what is there. I am sure he knows more than his sister.'

'Does he suspect me?'

'I do not think so. I cannot tell what he knows, but I believe, from the way he has with me, that he has more knowledge than we suppose. He has great and miraculous powers.'

'Pshaw!' scoffed Constantine. 'Do not be imposed on by his airs. He fancies that he has the gift of healing, but he is a quack and a mountebank.'

'You must not say that,' exclaimed Loveday, with some warmth. 'He is true to himself and to others.'

Constantine laughed. 'He imposes first on himself and then upon others. I thought you

had more common sense than to be deceived
by his pretensions. I'll tell you what happened
whilst I have been here. I went with Paul
one Sunday to Welcombe Church, and found it
crowded with an unusually large congregation.
All through the service it was clear the people
were thinking of something other than the
prayers and sermon. When the parson retired, then the churchwardens came up to the
Featherstone pew, and asked Paul to accompany them. So he went out, and all the
people lined the churchyard path, apparently
expecting something. They closed in after Paul
and the churchwardens, and followed them to
the church-house. " Us have got him at last,"
said one of the wardens. " The old enemy
be safe locked up in here," said the other.
" What do you mean? " asked Paul, much
puzzled. " Sure, Squire, us have caught the
devil, and locked him in. Nicolas Heyward,
there, found him in the road." We entered,
and there lay a black indiarubber ball on the
floor. " Nicolas Heyward took 'n up off the
road, not knowing what he was," said one of
the wardens; " and when he let 'n fall, then he
jumped and danced so high he was sure that

he'd laid hold on him then. So he said the Church Catechism right through, questions and all, and, thus fortified, he sent him on wi' his foot, till he got him into the church-house, and there he be." "Why," said Paul, "this is quite natural; it is not Satan, it is an indiarubber bouncing ball." Then he took it up and went out before all the congregation, and tried to explain its properties. Then he threw it down, and away it sprang over their heads, and the folk flew right and left; and where the ball fell no one ever saw. But all Welcombe parish believes that Squire Featherstone conjured the devil away.'[1]

'Mr. Featherstone did not encourage their superstition; he endeavoured to dispel it.'

'He could do no other, with me at his elbow. If I had not been present, there is no knowing to what hocus-pocus he might have had resort.'

'For shame, Constantine!'

'Well,' said he, with a laugh and shrug of his shoulders, 'it is an instance of the way in which the people encourage him in his craze;

---

[1] A true incident that occurred about forty years ago. The thing found was, however, not a ball, but a gutta-percha whip.

and he does nothing, as you have seen, to discourage them in their belief. Here, Loveday, give me the baby.'

He took the child in his arms and played with it. The little fellow laughed, and beat with his feet on his father's knees, and tried to stand and leap on them. Loveday had stuck little tufts of golden bachelor's-buttons down the front of his dress, and as Constantine danced him they fell out on his lap, and then on the ground about his feet, where he carelessly trod on them.

'He is like me, is he not, Loveday?' asked he.

'Yes, despotic as a Gaverock,' she replied.

'Tell me about home,' said Constantine. 'I have heard nothing since I left, and I cannot make inquiries. I have not had the chance of asking you. Is the old place just the same—and the old people, how are they?'

She told him about them. He was interested and moved by recollections, and sighed.

'It is very hard! You cannot understand my feelings. I wish again and again that I could go home and see them all. Now that I may not, I feel an almost uncontrollable desire to go. My father was rough, but, after all, Gerans and I had a very happy boyhood. How is Phœbus?'

'Phœbus belongs now to Rose.'

'She will not know how to manage him. I should like to slip back to Towan, by night, open the stable door, and gallop away on Phœbus. But it would not do; it cannot be. Oh, Loveday! I have imprisoned myself here. I dare not go anywhere, lest I should be stumbled upon and recognised by some one from our parts. I have come to hate this nook of the world. Look at those bachelor's-uttons—how scraggy they grow! Do you remember the plant in the Towan garden under the drawing-room window? I nearly committed myself one day when I was here with Juliot. She spoke of this very tuft, and said that she was fond of the golden flower. Then I laughed, and said I knew far finer shrubs of bachelor's-buttons. "You should see ours," I began; then recollected myself, and turned the colour of a peony.'

Loveday sighed.

'Look at this little fellow,' said Constantine. 'There is not a scrap of Featherstone in him,

I am glad to say; he has my nose, and my hair, and his eyes will, I think, be like mine—only one cannot tell of what colour a baby's eyes are. Loveday, was my father very angry when he heard about our marriage?'

'At first, but he soon cooled.'

'Ah! now that it is too late, I wish I had been brave and told him all. One is always wise after the event, when it is irrevocable. I hate my life here, with this weariful Paul Featherstone, solemn and dreamy, and in this cramped nook from which I can no more escape than a mouse from a trap. How is Bryony?'

'What, the black cow?'

'Yes. I remember her when she was a little calf. I was wont to give her sugar, and she was tame as a kitten, and ran after me and licked my hand. Whenever I came home from Padstow she ambled and jumped for joy. She had not forgotten me on my return from Exeter. I went through the yard when the cows were being brought in to be milked, and she broke away from the rest, and lowed, and rubbed her head against me, and licked my hand.'

'I heard Mrs. Gaverock say that Bryony gave more milk than two of the red Devons.'

'I care for nothing here, and for nobody——'

'Nobody!' exclaimed Loveday, looking round. 'Not this little fellow?'

'Oh, of course, I exclude him. If I ran away I should carry him with me. You must not condemn me for what I have done. All men make mistakes some time or other, only most are able to redress them somehow, and I cannot—that is the difference.' Then he handed the baby back to Loveday. He was tired of holding it, and of its jumps and pats on his checks. 'The little fellow goes to you quite readily, as if——' He checked himself. A constrained pause ensued. 'Were they very distressed at Towan when they thought I was dead?' he asked.

'It nigh on broke your dear mother's heart. She has never recovered the shock. She was off her head for a while, thinking of you as a child.'

'Ah! so was I off my head. If I had not been so, I would not have got into this cursed predicament. So Gerans is married, and has got Rose. Some fellows are born to luck. Why, she must be worth four or five hundred a year, and charming to boot. Gerans is a good fellow, but that is no reason why the skies should rain gold on him and pitch on me. I could be quite as good a fellow as he if circumstances allowed me. The saying is, " A poet is born, not made "; it is the reverse with a virtuous man—he is made, not born. How can a man be righteous when he is impecunious? A man must live. When you are drowning you catch at what you can to keep you afloat, and don't ask if the casks have paid the excise on which you are washed ashore. Was the " Mermaid " badly hurt ? '

Loveday was made uncomfortable by his conversation. She did not see his meanness, selfishness, and want of balance, but his talk fretted her wounded and suffering heart, she hardly knew why.

' Constantine,' she said, ' never mind about the " Mermaid." We have other matters that concern us more nearly. I think day and night about them, and it seems to me that there is no escape from the consequences this side the grave. We must do our duty, each going the straight road that opens before us, and spare others as much as we can.'

'Be easy,' he answered, with a tone of impatience ; 'I shall find a way out. A rabbit has more holes than one to his burrow. There is no knot that cannot be untied with patience.'

Loveday shook her head sadly. 'We are all enveloped in one cloud,' she said, ' and the cloud is so charged with lightning that some must be struck, and none can escape unsinged. You are bound to both Juliot and me—to both by the most sacred vows. My claim is the elder, and is the claim that the law would allow. Nevertheless, you are bound to her ; you made promises to her, and she put her life in your hands, trusting to them. You are bound to her by this mutual bond.' She bent over the child, which was falling asleep, and her tears dropped on its sweet, innocent face. 'The child itself has a strong claim on you by nature, though not by law. Why do you speak so lightly of rabbit holes, and taking your choice out of which you will run? You can leave neither Juliot nor me without breaking a tie one end of which is attached to your heart. You cannot leave either Juliot or me without giving one of us inexpressible pain. You have broken your mother's heart, you have broken mine, and—it is inevitable—you must break Juliot's. Yes, the saying is true: "The earth is strewn with potsherds"—the broken lives of us frail vessels of clay.'

'I suppose I shall have to leave Marsland,' said Constantine. 'I shall not be sorry. I am weary of my imprisonment here. I did what was wrong, and I repent. My conscience will not be easy till I have escaped from this false position. But whither am I to go? I have no money. I cannot return to Nankivel at Exeter or to Towan without giving some account of myself, and I am a bad hand at inventing lies. I have told enough since I came here, and every one of them has cut my throat as it came up.'

'Nevertheless, that is your best course. Return to your father, but tell no lies. Decline to say where you have been.'

'Yes! and then there will be hue-and-cry through the country after me. Paul will advertise me—full description given, and full account of how I was found. Then, what will happen?

Judge for yourself. No, Loveday, that will not answer.'

'You are bound to go,' said Loveday. 'That is a clear duty.'

'And safer for me,' added Constantine.

'But,' she went on, 'do not go yet. I must leave; I cannot remain under the same roof with you and Juliot. I cannot visit my cousin, as I do not know where she is. You must bestir yourself to find some situation for me; otherwise I shall leave without knowing whither I am going. My position here is insupportable.'

Just then Juliot came into the garden, and seeing the two together on the bench talking, she clapped her hands, and called over her shoulder to her brother:

'Paul! Paul! come here. I am so glad! John is reconciled at last to Loveday.'

'I am rejoiced that his eyes are opened to acknowledge worth where it is found,' said Paul, entering.

'Do you know, Loveday,' explained Juliot, 'that Mr. Rock was quite prejudiced against you? He did not know you, and I think he was afraid that you would steal away baby's heart from me. Now that you have had a talk together you will have come to like each other —I am so delighted!'

'Dinner is ready,' Juliot said, when Constantine stood up, greatly confused.

Then all went together into the hall. Constantine had not dined with Loveday since her recovery; he had kept away at Stanbury. Now, as he sat at table, he looked from her to Juliot, and from Juliot back to Loveday. There could be little question which was the most attractive of the two women to whom he was bound. Juliot had the simplicity of a child in her face; that of Loveday was full of intelligence, and the sweetness bred of pain. They were both pleasant looking, but Loveday was the most beautiful.

'After all,' said Constantine to himself, 'I do love my first wife, and I do not care particularly for the second. Confound that fool, Paul, for throwing his sister at my head!'

CHAPTER XLIII.

BETWEEN TWO HEAVENS.

'I HAVE a plan, a beautiful plan,' said Juliot, when the early dinner was ended. 'The day is so perfect, the wind is off shore, and the sea is so still, that I have set my mind on Loveday having a paddle on the water. What do you say, Paul? Will you take the oars? From you, Loveday, I will allow no refusal. The air on the sea, the sun, the sparkling water, will do you much good, and bring colour to your pale cheeks.'

'Which boat shall we take?' asked Paul. 'I suppose Rock will take an oar as well.'

'Oh, no!' exclaimed Juliot, eagerly, 'John is not going, nor am I. That is, we will stroll with you as far as the beach, but I shall have baby in my arms, and I am not going to sea with him. You will probably stay out longer than the young gentleman will approve, so I

retain John to assist me in carrying him home.
If he is amiable, we will await you on the sand
and let the fine fellow play with the shingle ;
if he be overcome with *ennui*, John and I will
transport him home.'

'I think it would do the child good to be
rowed about in the bay,' said Constantine.

'My dear John, you must leave me to decide what is good for my boy.   When he is six
months or a year older I will not object.   The
air would be too strong for his lungs now, or
his lungs might be too strong for those in the
boat.   He is capricious, and when he wills
spoils the best sport.'

' As you choose,' said Constantine.

Paul Featherstone was well content to meet
his sister's wishes.   Loveday was grateful for
the thought and kindness ; Constantine alone
appeared dissatisfied with the proposal, though
he did not actively oppose it.   The four, Juliot
carrying the baby, descended the valley towards
the shore of Marsland Mouth.

'Do not wait for us,' said Juliot.   'Push
on, Paul, with Miss Penhalligan, and seize the
day in its splendour.   My fine gentleman de-
tains me ; he wishes to touch everything he sees,

and what he touches he puts into his mouth. He is an experimental philosopher. Well, sir, what is your opinion of dandelion? Will it serve as a pickle? The flies are tiresome, are they, Constantine the little? John, dear, fetch me some large bracken leaves, that I may arrange them about his hat to drive away the tormentors. There, sir, is King Charles's oak in the bracken stalk, where your father has cut athwart. It does not interest you now. Wait a few years, and then you will be hunting for the meanings of the cabalistic characters in the fern-stalk yourself.'

Constantine assisted Paul in running the boat to the water; then Loveday was handed in. Featherstone removed his coat, and took an oar. 'You will not take the other?' asked he of Constantine.

'No, Paul,' said Juliot, 'John remains with me.'

'I don't know that,' said Constantine, perversely. 'Hold hard, Featherstone, I will join you.'

But Paul thrust off from land, and left his brother-in-law on the beach, with a moody brow and a dissatisfied grumble.

' Come to me, John,' said Juliot. 'Do you not see? You men are so dull : I do not want a third to spoil that little water-party.'

'Why should I spoil it?' he asked, impatiently.

'Oh, John! you think me simple, but I am shrewder in some matters than you.'

Her words, instead of allaying, aggravated his discontent. He paced the sands, and looked after the receding boat with an angry scowl.

' John, what is the matter?'

' I ought to have been at Stanbury to-day, not fooling here.'

Paul rowed Loveday well out from shore. The sky was perfectly serene, and as the wind was from the east and blew over the cliffs, the sea was unruffled for some way out ; indeed, in the bay, it was quite still. The beauty of colour in the water was indescribable. The sea on the north-west coast is so deep, the rocks rising precipitously out of many fathoms of water, that it is wholly void of earthy particles, and is transparent almost as an atmosphere and blue as the sky overhead.

The sea, though it did not form waves, and

to the eye was still, yet heaved with the swell from the ocean ; but the effect was soothing— it was as though the sea were breathing in sweet sleep under the rays of the summer sun.

That the sea was not altogether still was also evident from the line of white about the rocks, a precipitous cliff that formed the horn of the bay dividing it from Welcombe Mouth. The surf was, however, nothing to-day compared to what it usually was over and about the slate rocks there. Loveday looked up at the sky, and then down into the sea. It seemed as though the boat were hanging between two equally deep, blue, and tranquil heavens.

'You are almost disposed to doubt which is the real heaven,' said Paul ; 'many look for it below, instead of above, yet there is one beneath as well as one above—bright, beautiful, peaceful, so long as it reflects the upper heaven. Shall I tell you what is the occasion of breaker and foam and wreck and ruin? It is the setting of the wind inland, instead of off the shore. Which is an allegory.' Then he pulled more vigorously, and shot round a rock beyond sight of those on the beach. The gulls were fluttering around, flashing like snow-flakes. Loveday put her fingers over the side, and let the clear water flow between them. As the boat moved a soft air fanned her face, but failed when Paul suddenly shipped his oars and allowed the boat to float and heave on the sea as it listed.

Then he put his hand in his waistcoat pocket and drew forth a piece of silver paper, which he unfolded, and from it took a gold ring attached to a thread of blue silk, and handed it in his palm to Loveday.

'Madam,' said he, 'I return you what was yours, found by me under circumstances I need not detail. That it is connected with your trouble, I am well assured. Of your secret grief I know nothing, and I desire to know no more than you choose to tell. But, madam, I am moved to ask you to confide somewhat in me. You are alone, and without a counsellor; I might help you, and I trust I could tender you consolation also.'

He had found the ring suspended by its silken thread to a frond of maidenhair fern beside the spring in the lane. Loveday had, indeed, missed it, and been uneasy at its loss,

and quite unconscious that she had cast it from
her in a sleep-walk.

The faint colour that had come into her
cheeks fanned by the sea air died away, and a
cloud came over her eyes. She trembled when
she took the ring from his hand; she said
nothing for some minutes, but her bosom
heaved, not with the even swell of the sea at
that moment, but as it heaves at the coming
on of a storm. Presently she raised her eyes
to the face of Paul Featherstone, and said in a
low, but distinct voice : ' It belongs to me.
You have a right to know more. I have been
married, and have lost my husband.'

' Lost——'

' Lost at sea.'

' Your happiness was of short duration ? '

' My happiness ! '

She said no more, but her tone told him
how very short, how very slight, the happiness
had been.

He put the oars into the water again, and
rowed on, outward, to where the wind coming
over the cliffs touched and roughened the
surface—but the touch was light and the
roughness little. Holding the oars in the
water, or raising them and letting the clear

drops run off the blades, using no exertion, but seeing that the tide did not carry the boat further, Paul paused, and looking gravely at Loveday he said, ' You have no home, no one to care for you, to protect you from trouble, to shield you from harm ; no one to whom to confide your sorrows, and from whom to accept consolation. From the moment that I found your ring, I suspected your story, and——' He hesitated, drew a long breath, and said, ' I have desired an opportunity of asking you to accept from me that of which you are bereaved.'

Loveday looked at him at first with uneasiness, then with alarm.

' The time must come, and come quickly, when my brother-in-law will leave Marsland, and take up his residence at Stanbury with his wife and child. Stanbury is theirs, and, somehow, Mr. Rock and I do not agree together quite as well as I should wish. I have nothing to say against him, but our opinions and feelings are not harmonious, and it is best that he should go to his own house, where he is master. And now, madam, I venture, very humbly, and knowing my own deficiencies and your transcendent excellence, to entreat you——'

'Oh, stay, stay!' exclaimed Loveday, in tones of distress. She clasped her hands, and entreated, 'Oh, Mr. Featherstone, I beseech you, say no more!'

He obeyed, he rowed harder, turned the head of the boat landwards, and was silent. Loveday sat speechless, with her hands pressed to her bosom. The cup of bitterness that had been given her was not drained to the dregs. She must be a cause of disappointment and grief to the good, courteous, and kind man who had led hitherto a life free from heart-ache.

After a long silence he said, whilst still rowing :

'I must not allow this interview to pass without making myself clearly understood, without assuring myself that you do not mistake my meaning. I look on you with such respect, such tender regard, that I should be most happy to place my life, my fortune, my name at your feet.'

'It cannot be,' answered Loveday, profoundly agitated, gasping for breath.

'Tell me this,' he said, 'you do not love another?'

'No,' she replied, after a moment's thought ;

'I think of none but the husband I have lost.'

'But he is lost!' exclaimed Paul.

Loveday covered her eyes, and bowed her face on her knees.

The sun was declining now, and its rays gilt the cliffs; the boat was out of the rougher water, under the lee of the coast again. The gulls were screaming and chattering, boldly diving near the boat, and coming up with fish, and dashing on to wing again with a splash of water.

'Madam,' said Paul Featherstone, 'why can you not be happy at Marsland? A quiet corner of a quiet world, where there is nothing to distress from without or from within—almost too quiet for our good, maybe—perhaps too still to last without a ruffle. My sister loves you, and would gladly receive you. Of myself I will say nothing, save this, that the whole desire of my life would be to make you happy.'

'You are so good, so generous,' said Loveday, 'that it goes to my heart to refuse you, but—I cannot, I cannot.'

'Regard for the dead,' continued Paul, 'is

just and good ; but do not let the dead stand between you and happiness. The dead do not return from the deep of the sea to cut you off from home and rest and love. They do not haunt us, after they are dead, to forbid us forming new friendships and relationships. By all means be faithful to the memory of him you have lost, but, believe me, he in Paradise will rejoice, if he ever loved you, to see that his poor storm-beaten dove is offered a sheltering cot.'

She could not speak, the power to answer was gone from her, so great was her despair.

'I am in no hurry,' Paul went on. 'I will wait for you patiently two or three years, till your fresh grief has abated. If I trouble you now, it is only because I am eager to save you from fresh trials.'

'Oh, how good, how kind to me!' said Loveday. 'And I seem so ungrateful! Oh, Mr. Featherstone, believe me, there is no man on earth whom I respect as I respect you. There is no man on earth from whom I could obtain better guidance, more strength, holier comfort. Be my friend, my guide—if I may ask this ; but ask for nothing further. It cannot be. Indeed, indeed.' She fell on her knees in the boat, and put her hands to her brow. 'I cannot explain myself. I shall go mad. It cannot be.'

'Madam,' said Paul, 'I fear I have been too hasty. Your sorrow is too recent. I can wait. I apologise for having spoken ; I will transgress no more. Have no fear. Endeavour to forget the rash words that I have addressed to you. It grieves me to the heart that I have troubled you. You have asked me to be your friend ; I am content to stand in that capacity to you. Consider me for ever after as your friend, who has your interests and welfare near his heart ; I am honoured beyond my deserts to be so re-garded. I was premature in speaking, because I thought that the time would shortly come when Mr. Rock and I would part—he to go to Stanbury, I to remain here. But I will master my repugnance—that is, I mean I will think the best I can of him, excuse him as far as I can, and bear with what it costs me a struggle to endure, for your sake. I am sorry to speak thus of my own brother-in-law, but I cannot avoid it. I am disappointed ; he is hardly what I supposed him to be. But there, I will say no more on this topic, which is painful to me, and only touched on to explain my temerity

in addressing you as I have to-day. Madam,
we are at the shore. Allow me to offer you
my hand to disembark. On some future occasion, it may be far away, I shall dare to offer it
you again—then to embark on a cruise as still
and untossed as that to-day, to float with me
between two heavens.'

She made no answer, but stepped ashore.
He drew the boat up and secured it; then
offered her his arm, but she declined it. Constantine and Juliot were no longer on the beach;
the evening was settling down, and the dew
falling, so the mother had carried baby home.
As Loveday walked without speaking at Paul's
side, he also was silent. She thought of his
words, ' floating between two heavens.' She
had been cast out of the rest and serenity of
one, and a second had been opened and offered
to her that day, into which she could not enter.
Peace, happiness, security, love, were no more
for her; she could no more recover the heaven
she had lost, nor reach another. She still loved
Constantine, but she had lost respect for him.
Even if she were to condone the past, a home
with him would never be a happy home; the
recollection of his treachery, his desertion, must

penetrate and poison it. The iron had entered into her soul, and could never be extracted; and the wound could not be salved over by his hand.

Paul regretted his precipitation, but did not lose hope. Surely, in time, the living would take the place of the dead in her thoughts. He resolved to behave towards her as he had done hitherto—in no way to force his attentions upon her, to embarrass and pain her.

She was tired ascending the hill, which was very steep, and Paul cut her a stout ash staff, on which to lean, as she declined his arm.

At last they reached the house. At the entrance of the first court under the gatehouse Paul said, in a low tone:

'One final word, and I will trouble you no more with my attentions. Have you noticed the scroll that adorns the old sun-dial in the garden? Upon it stands the legend, "I wait upon the sun." I am like that dial. I will not be dispirited by rejection, by cloud, by wintry shadow. I will live in hope, and will wait upon the sun.'

CHAPTER XLIV.

FLED.

THE proposal of Paul Featherstone had greatly increased Loveday's uneasiness. She could not remain longer at Marsland, placed between a husband who did not acknowledge her, and was married to another, and an honourable, sincere man who sought her as his wife. If her position was intolerable before, it was made more so by the event of that day. She could not, she must not, remain. She had, indeed, accepted Constantine's undertaking to find her a place, but some time must elapse before the place was found, and Constantine was not a man of energy to bestir himself.

She was impatient, moreover, to communicate with her brother and with her friends at Towan, and relieve them from the suspense in which she was aware they must be, not know-

ing what had become of her. She was not
angry with Constantine—she was disappointed
with him, and her faith in him was more com ·
pletely wrecked than her faith in Dennis. She
was not jealous of Juliot—she loved and pitied
her. For Paul she felt great regard, and some
awe. She could not remain at Marsland,
because the conflicting feelings constantly
roused in her bosom were more than she could
bear. The strain was never off her. She was
conscious of a craving in her soul for rest, a
longing to be away, where she should no longer
see her husband, her rival, the child that was
his but not hers, the man who sought of her
what she could not give him. There was not
one of the household that did not cause her
a pang. Hitherto, Paul, and he alone, had
been a comfort to her. In his society and
conversation she could, in a measure, escape
from her cares It was so now no longer.
His company would embarrass her; he would
be another to fill her with nervous alarm.

That night, when she retired to her room,
she considered what was to be done. She was
without one person to whom she could apply
for advice. She was forced to be everything to

herself. More strength was required of her than she was endowed with—strength of will, strength of judgment, strength of nerve, physical power.

How long would it be before Constantine advertised? He had asked no particulars as to what sort of a situation she needed; he had offered to advertise in his careless, inconsiderate manner, and days might elapse before he fulfilled his undertaking; and, after that, more time must pass before answers arrived, and more still before final arrangements were come to. Thus weeks might drag out before she got away. She had not the courage to contemplate this. She might recover her health if away from the sights and voices that troubled her, but a few more days among them would cast her back on the bed of sickness. She *must* get away. Her soul hungered, ached, strained for escape.

What excuse could she offer for leaving? She had been treated with exceptional kindness. To leave would savour of ingratitude. Yet Paul's offer furnished the excuse. She might make it her plea that she could no longer with delicacy remain in the house of the man whom

she had refused. He would understand this,
and explain her conduct to Juliot. This consideration decided her. She would leave at
once. Instead of going to bed, she remained
up all night packing her box, reserving from
it only those few things which she would need
at once, and which she could carry in her
reticule. Then, in the early hours of the
morning, she stole downstairs, unfastened the
hall door, and left Marsland. She took with
her the staff Paul had cut the evening before
and placed in her hand. That was the only
thing she carried from Marsland with her,
except her painful secret.

The morning air was fresh; the birds were
singing already, although the sun was not yet
risen. There was light in the sky, as there
always is at midsummer, and the light was
growing, for in another hour the sun would rise.
Away in the north-west the Lundy lighthouse
was winking; aloft was one star, fading. She
hurried away from the house with beating
heart, for as she passed out of the porch she
heard the plaintive wail of the baby. It was
cutting teeth, and fretful in the night, waking
with a start, in a terror, and crying out and

sobbing. Juliot also was awake, sitting up in her bed, and soothing the infant, speaking caressingly to it, kissing its little hands and fiery cheek.

Paul's dog came to her bounding, fawning, and asking to be patted, addressed, and taken a walk. Loveday had some difficulty in persuading him not to attend her.

She left the court and the avenue, and descended the hill to the spring. The water was dark now; neither diamonds nor pearls fell over the rock, and the maidenhair fern leaf was not visible in the gloom of the hedge. Loveday stood one moment by the spring, holding the ash root, recalling that first terrible interview; then she put her hands to the water and caught it in her palms, and drank. The freshness of the air and of the fountain invigorated her, and she pushed on.

Of the country she knew nothing. She had but a vague recollection of the way by which she had come from Stratton. She remembered a high road, and then lanes—intricate, winding, innumerable. But she had a general idea as to the direction she must take. She had resolved to go to Stratton, and thence make her way by coach to Launceston, where she would remain

till she had decided on her future course. She
must keep the sea on her right hand—that she
knew. In course of time she must reach
Stratton or Bude Haven. Bude was only three
miles from Stratton. Should she reach Bude
first, she must strike inland for the town of
Stratton. That formed the substance of what
she knew. Unfortunately, she was ignorant of
the structure (orography, we should call it now,
but the word was unknown then) of the land ;
and, consequently, instead of striking inland, due
east, till she hit the high road on the backbone
of the moor, she hugged the coast, and lost herself
among winding lanes, among hills and valleys,
which only a goat could scramble up directly ;
where the lanes zigzagged, and dodged, and
shifted direction at every bowshot she went. The
hills, even when ascended at a slant, are mere
scrambles, most exhausting to a strong man, and
Loveday was worn with sickness and without
food. She came upon neither farmhouse nor
village inn. The sun rose, and struck on her
back with scorching heat as she toiled up the hills.
She stood still, and wiped the perspiration from
her brow, whilst she leaned on Paul's stick. She
was sick and faint with hunger. From weak-

ness, the tears came into her eyes and mingled
with the drops that fell from her forehead.
When she had a steep hill to descend, her feet
failed her ; she leaned heavily on the staff, and
her ankles turned ; she had not the strength to
stay herself from falling ; and when she stood
still, her limbs quivered with convulsive mus-
cular trembling—the fruit of over-exertion. If
she could have found a farm she would have
asked for bread and a cup of milk, if she had
lighted on an inn she would have ordered a
meal ; but she was out of the region of houses,
passing now over gorse-strewn moors, then
through oak coppice. The wild strawberries
were ripe, but too small to satisfy her. On
reaching the bottom of a glen, overcome by
weariness, she crept into a little wood of dwarf
oak, laid herself down in the bracken under
the shade, and, before she was aware that she
was sleepy, sank into unconsciousness.

Whilst she lay thus hidden, slumbering from
exhaustion of mind and body, the day changed.
The burning rays of the sun had been those
which precede a storm. Clouds rose, covered
the sky, and cut off the heat and light of the
sun. A cold wind wailed through the valley,

and whistled among the oak leaves of the coppice. Loveday slept on. Her tiredness after the sleepless night, and the weariness of her walk, and the exhaustion consequent on want of food, had cast her into a paralysing slumber, in which she neither heard nor felt— did not even dream. She did not wake till the storm burst; then she was cold, shivering, and bewildered. She came forth from the dripping wood to see scuds of rain drive by, filling the valley with flying drifts that concealed every object. The lightning flashed, and the thunder boomed, but not very near; and the lightning, though vivid, was not forked and distinct. The wind roared up the valley, and on its breath carried the growl of the angry sea which it was lashing into fury. Uncertain where she was, and in what direction she had to go, Loveday ascended the hill she had last come down and emerged on a moor, where she lost her way, and found herself near the ragged edge of a cliff that projected into space illimitable, like the last hour of life. In her alarm she took the opposite direction, but could make out no road. Tracks there were, trodden by cattle, that led nowhere. The valleys below

were filled with eddying vapour and driving
rain. She was drenched. The water ran up
her sleeve from the staff she held. The wind
caught her ribbons and made of them instru-
ments of shrill screaming music. The water
came as in sheets from her brow over her eyes,
blinding her, and the moisture soaked her
bosom. Her skirts clung to her limbs as though
they had been dipped in a river.

She seated herself under a ragged scrap of
hedge, made of stones and clay, that the cattle
had scrambled over and trodden down till it
resembled the jaw of an old woman with a few
fangs standing up. Under one of these she
crouched, with a thorn-bush stretching above
her landwards like a streamer. The wind
howled and screeched through the twigs, and
curled round the corners and lashed at her wet
skirts, and beat her in the face with splashes of
sea foam.

She could not sit there, worn out with
hunger, with knees that trembled with fatigue,
numbed with the wet that penetrated everywhere. She stood up with an involuntary
moan, and staggered forwards.

Surely the evening was setting in, the light

was perceptibly becoming less. The thunder rolled away and muttered in the distance, but the rain continued to fall. Loveday looked up, and around—there was no rent anywhere in the clouds.

If she could but find the road again, the road must lead to some habitation. Little by little she would push on till she reached a cottage. Any house, however humble, would suffice. Driven inland by the wind, holding to the staff to prevent herself from being blown over, picking her way among gorse-bushes, she reached at length a rough stone wall, and was obliged to turn down it towards the valley before she could find a gate. Then she saw by it what in the dialect of the country is called a tallat— that is, a shed, wattled and roofed with gorse-bushes, and with an open door. She was thankful for the shelter, and crept in; but the floor was dirty, it had been trodden by horses, and the water had entered from the ground outside. She went to the farther end, by the manger, where it was drier, and laid herself down there. She put her hands to her face to wipe the wet from her eyes, and she took the cold, soaked bonnet from her head, and tried to rest against the side, but the prickles of the gorse pierced her. There was nothing she could lean against except one rough piece of wreck wood, that supported the manger. Against this she sat, upright, with her face to the entrance through which the wan light entered, and the wind and rain eddied. She had thrown up her sodden bonnet into the manger; discoloured drops fell from it, stained with the dye in the once pretty ribbons.

At first she felt warm in this sheltered tallat— compared with outside it was warm; but Loveday had carried the chill in with her in her soaked garments, and she soon began to feel numbed. Then she heard a scampering without, and some wild moor ponies appeared at the entrance, roans with bleached manes. They stood in the doorway and stared at her, then plunged away, then returned. One more daring than the rest entered, but when Loveday spoke it threw up its heels and dashed forth again, snorting and whinnying.

This was notice for her to leave. She dared not remain longer, wet to the bone, in the tallat. But when she tried to rise her limbs were so stiff that she could scarcely move them, and

her knees when she rose failed under her. She
considered that if horses and an enclosure were
there, there must be a farm near ; but her heart
sank. She doubted if she would have strength
to reach it.

.   .   .   .   .

Constantine was sitting that same evening
in the kitchen at Stanbury with old Carwithen.

A fire was smouldering on the hearth, the
wood was from a wreck, and it gave forth the
peculiar odour which comes from wood that
has been long immersed in sea-water; the
afternoon was so stormy and damp that a fire
was pleasant. They had the kettle over the
fire boiling, and on the table tumblers and a
bottle of spirits. Constantine had left Marsland the evening before, after seeing Juliot
safe home with the baby, and had slept the
night at Stanbury. During the morning he
had been about the farm, but had been driven
in by the storm. Accordingly he spent his
afternoon with old Carwithen and hot rum-and-
water. A good deal of rum was drunk at
Stanbury, and not one drop of it had paid
duty.

'I'll tell y' what it be, your honour,' said

Carwithen, knocking the ashes out of his pipe against the side of the fireplace. 'It is my opinion that I put you in the way of becoming master of Stanbury, and I expect some consideration for it. If you be coming to live here along with madam, what is to become of me? Am I to turn out o' Stanbury and go down to Featherstone's Kitchen and live there? I've been long enough here to like a better house. I put you up to getting Stanbury, but I did not reckon on your turning me out.'

'Is it not reasonable?' asked Constantine, impatiently. 'This house is mine—at least, it is my wife's, and here we shall live, as we ought. I am sick of Marsland; I'll no longer stay there with that canting fool, Featherstone; I'll come here. Here I shall be master in my own house, and, whether you like it or not, you must turn out. I will give you employment on the land.'

'At what wage?'

'At an ordinary day-labourer's wage.'

'I am not to have my hind's wage?'

'Of course not. I shall be here to manage my own affairs. I shall not need a hind. I shall not pay more than I am obliged.'

'So, this is what I receive for putting you up to getting the place!'

'How can you talk so foolishly! You have had nothing to do with me and my marriage. I am not a fool. How the wind roars! It will blow in the window. The water is coming in through the leadwork, and driving in under the door. We shall be swamped if this continues.'

'Master,' said Carwithen, surlily, 'you're well enough and friendly wi' a fellow as long as he serves your purpose, but as soon as you think you can do without him, you're ready to kick him aside with no compunction. That's not Scripture.'

'You have no claim upon me at all. I shall pay such men as I want, and such wages as are reasonable. I shall not want a hind when I am here myself, therefore I shall not keep one. If you are not content to take a labourer's pay you may look out for a hind's place elsewhere. Hark! Good Heaven! what is that?'

A blow at the door had startled him, as though some heavy body had fallen against it.

'Nothing but the wind,' said Carwithen.

' I've heard the wind beat at the windows that
you could have sworn it was some one outside
striking them with his hands.   Satan be called
the Prince of the Power of the Air.   When
he heard you threatening to cut me down
he were inclined to be in and strangle you for
your wickedness.'

' If a man is not to look after his own interests,' said Constantine, ' no one else will look
after them for him.'

' True for you,' said Carwithen, ' but a
man's best interests don't always lie in using
short measure in dealing with others and long
measure in dealing with self.   Master Paul
Featherstone at Marsland will be better served
than you at Stanbury, for he measures long to
others and short to self.'

' I think it is time for you to go and see
after the cattle,' said Constantine.   ' Finish
your glass of grog first.'

' I'll do that without invitation,' said Carwithen.   And when the old man had put his
pipe on the mantelshelf and drained his glass,
he threw a sack over his shoulders, put a
south-wester on his head, grasped a staff, and
went to the door.

'Upon my word,' said he, 'the wind be beating against it so that I doubt if I can shut the door again. Come you here, master, and put your shoulder to it after I'm outside.'

Then Carwithen opened the door, and the wind and rain rioted into the kitchen, blowing the log into a sudden blaze, and whirling the white wood ashes in an eddy on the hearth.

'Good Lord!' cried the old man, 'what have we here?'

Upon the threshold lay the body of a woman, soaked with rain; she had apparently reached the door and fallen unconscious on the step as she tried to knock for admission. Her failing powers had carried her so far, and there deserted her.

Constantine was behind Carwithen, with his head down, against the wind, that blew his hair about. The old man knelt, and turned the face of the woman towards the light.

'My God!' gasped Constantine, and smote his brow. 'What is to be done? Loveday! Loveday!'

CHAPTER XLV.

FEATHERSTONE'S KITCHEN.

In a hollow of the moor over which poor Loveday had wandered in the storm without finding shelter was a cottage ; the roof was of turf, and so low that it was invisible till one was close upon it. It had but a single face, and that was turned, contrary to the invariable custom, towards the sea. All the other sides were banked up with peat, out of which the grass grew rankly, so that no one coming on the house would suppose it was a cabin inhabited by human beings, and not a gigantic rabbit warren.

In front of this hovel, on a bench, sat Loveday and a girl. The girl was Tamsin Carwithen, the daughter of the old hind at Stanbury. She lived in this odd turf house, and earned a few shillings by watching the

cattle turned out to graze on the down. She
was a young woman of thirty, with strongly-
marked features, a rough, uncivilised girl,
almost as wild as the colt that had claimed the
tallat into which Loveday had intruded.

' How came I here?' said Loveday. ' I
remember nothing.'

' I reckon you don't,' answered Thomasine
—Tamsin, as she was called. ' You was nigh
melted right away, you must have been out
and about in that storm. My word! it came
down proper solid water sheets.'

' Where was I found?'

' At Stanbury. You'd got so far and could
go no further, I reckon. Father found you
over the drexil (threshold) when he went to
open the door.'

' But who is your father?'

' Old Dick Carwithen, sure enough. Who
other?'

' He took me into Stanbury?'

' Ees, he did. He and the young Squire.'

' Who?'

' Squire Rock. Father and he were sitting,
smoking and talking and drinking sperrits and
water together, and they heard a sort of bang

agin' the door, but they took no particular
heed. The wind were hammering that power-
ful on window and door, they thought it the
wind. But, after a bit, father up and out after
the cattle, and there he found you, as I said, in a
faint, and wet as seaweed, on the drexil. So
he called to the Squire, and the Squire and he
carried you in, and mother, her came, and
they took you to the best bedroom, and there
the men left you, and mother undressed you,
and put on you warm blankets, and set a hot
brick to your feet, and made some rabbit
broth, and fed you with it, and last of all you
was dressed in my clothes and brought here.'

'But why here?'

'Sure enough, I cannot tell. The master
wouldn't allow you to bide in Stanbury. He
said, No, you must be took to Featherstone's
Kitchen.'

'To what?'

'To this place, for certain; this be Featherstone's Kitchen. Not, you know, Squire
Featherstone's kitchen to Marsland. Lord
bless you! don't think that. There be reasons
why this house is called Featherstone's Kitchen,
and there be others like it, I'm told, further

down the coast, right away to Land's End, but about here I know of none but this. It don't take its name after Squire Paul, bless your heart! It was christened after his uncle, who was a mighty rough sort of a man, very fond of the sea, and made it his pleasure to dare the gaugers. There be queer talk of he, I can tell you. I've nothing agin' him; he were a useful man in his time, he dug out this here Kitchen, and it serves its purpose now as well as then. I've heard tell that old Featherstone were here one day, sitting on a cask, when in at the door came a couple of sheriff's officers to take him. "My men," said he, and he took a pistol in his hand, "I'm sitting on a keg of gunpowder. I don't care a hang for my life, nor half a hang for yours. If you don't sheer off at once, I'll discharge the contents of the pistol into this here keg I be sitting on." Sure as cows have calves, and not calves cows, the sheriff's officers did sheer off.'

'But why was I brought here?' again asked Loveday.

'The young Squire would have it,' answered the girl. 'As soon as ever they seed there was life in you, then he gave father and mother

no rest, but swore you should not stay and be
nursed at Stanbury. Naught would please him
but that you was taken to the Kitchen. So
to the Kitchen you was took, and in the Kitchen
you be, leastways, a sitting in front of him ' (it).

Loveday was pained and surprised.

' I reckon,' Tamsin continued, ' he were a-
thinking of his missus. The master is married,
you know, to Squire Featherstone's sister. The
property be hers, not his. I've heard my father
tell that it be that tightly tied up that the
master can't lay a finger to it, can't sell a tree
off it, or an acre out of it. I reckon, all the
money belongs to Madam, and none to he ;
which must be as galling to a man as riding in
market on a lady's saddle. Well, it seems to
me, it stands this way. He thought his missus
might be jealous, hearing there was a leddy
staying at Stanbury, and he so much there
and not much at Marsland. If you larrup a
donkey with a bunch of thistles he'll not eat a
mouthful of thistles never after, he takes a dis-
taste to the sight of them. So I reckon it may
be with men, when they've a wife about 'em,
a-scratching and a-stinging, they take ever after
a sort of disgust to the sight of petticoats.

Women are jealous creatures, it is their nature. Mother told me that the young Squire laid it on her and father as hard as he could, they was not to say a word to nobody about you. He had you brought here where nobody would see you and none be the wiser, and run about telling tales and making of scandal. Squire Rock were mighty particular that you should be well cared for. You was to have chicken and rabbit broth, and wine, and wear my Sunday clothes, and mother's flannel petticoat, and have a hot bottle in your bed, and red currant jelly, and just anything one could think of to make a leddy happy and contented.'

Loveday sat silent, looking seaward and musing. Presently she found an explanation of Constantine's conduct which satisfied her, as it did not show him to be heartless. He had doubtless considered that she had escaped from Marsland with the intention of hiding herself. She could not remain concealed at Stanbury, therefore he had removed her to the cottage where she would be seen by no one, and where she might remain for many days without her hiding-place being discovered.

'If you'll come with me,' said Thomasine,

E 2

'I'll show you round the Kitchen. This be a queer place, sure enough, to those as is unacquainted with the like. The old Rover Featherstone, as he were called, he dursn't dispose of his goods too near to Marsland, though he had a store there, so he had a cave scooped out in the rock here, in our cottage. Mind you this bit o' land didn't belong to he. My grandfather were a squatter on it, and nobody said him nay. My grandfather was glad enough to oblige Red Featherstone in anything, so he helped to have a hole dug in the rock from our inner wood store. Squire Paul be another kind of man altogether. He have his fancies, and Red Featherstone had his. Men's tastes differ—some are all for religion, and some for wickedness; some can eat mussels, and others can't. I've known a man blown up and nigh strangled by eating of a dish of mussels which were innocent to another's stomach. It's just the same with smuggling, and wrecking, and drinking. They suited Red Featherstone's stomach, and they don't agree with Squire Paul. We ain't all constituted alike, praises be! Father ain't a dainty man. He can do with all sorts, pick a bit of Scripture, and then pick a bit of smuggling ; he can combine Gospel and drink, and curdle neither, but make a sort of junket out of 'em, which is a gift. Praises be ! If you will come along of me, I'll show y' a path in the face of the cliff down to the Cove. You see I keep a pair o' donkeys on the down. They can scramble up and down the cliffs, and are as sure-footed as a fly. When a boat comes into Marsland Mouth then they send the kegs over here in a row-boat, if weather permits, if not on the backs of donkeys. Bless your heart ! not on mine. All the farmers round about keep donkeys and lend 'em for the purpose. The smugglers take 'em, and no questions are asked. The farmers are pleased to help and loan 'em. But if a boat can be run to our Cove, then my beasts go down the cliff and bring up on their backs what sperits and other things are for this neighbourhood, and I store them away in Featherstone's Kitchen. So all the kitchens along the coast are supplied ; I dispose of the sperits and take the money, and so all parties are accommodated, which is a provision of nature, beautiful to think on, sure enough.'

'Have you never been married ?' asked Loveday.

'Never,' answered Thomasine, sorrowfully.
'That's the only real drawback to a place like
this. It's so out of the way you don't get a
fair start with other girls. It is not as if the
men will come after you, it is you must go
after them. Men are much like snipe in their
flight, and a straight shot from the shoulder
won't bring them down; you must allow for
their dipping. It is only the old and heavy
chaps as whirr up under your feet and go level
away like a partridge. And yet,' continued
Thomasine, 'I ain't sure that I shan't come in
to the goal and get the prize before others that
have started before me, and used more exertion
in the running. You see, Miss, the race for a
husband among us maidens is very much like a
race in sacks at a fair. There be a deal of hin-
drance and impediment, but along we go. It
is she as takes the littlest steps and minds to
keep the sack up about her neck as will come
in at last, not they as makes the big jumps and
is most fiery eager. They go down on their
noses pretty smart, and lie about like potatoes
turned out of a garden. It is shuffling on, not
leaps, as does it.'

The talkative girl was interrupted by the

appearance of Constantine, who came over the down towards the cottage.

Thomasine at once retired into the hovel. Constantine greeted Loveday with restraint ; he feared the eyes and ears of Thomasine, and he drew Loveday from the front of the cottage, away to the edge of the cliff, where they were beyond earshot.

' Loveday,' said he, ' I am glad you are better. You have no conception how anxious and distressed I have been. But what can have induced you to come to Stanbury? What more likely than such a course to arouse suspicion ? '

' I did not intend it,' she answered, meekly. ' I ran away from Marsland. I could not remain there longer——'

' Why not? I told you I would look out for some situation for you. You ought to have remained.'

' I could not, Con,' she said gently, but firmly. ' I will tell you why. I was there in a wrong position. I was there as an unmarried woman, and Mr. Featherstone has asked me ——' She faltered.

' I understand,' said Constantine, testily ;

'well, what of that? You refused him. It will do him good. He has his own way too much. His sister worships him, kneels before him in an adoring attitude, and that has turned his head. I am glad to hear he has had his nose tweaked. It will draw some of the fantastic humours out of him.'

'After that I could not stay.'

'Why not? I didn't ask you to stay long. Don't you see that by your conduct you are exciting suspicion? You think only of yourself, Loveday, and have no consideration for me. You should have stayed on a few days, then have given a formal notice, said that your health would not allow you to undertake the duties, and gone, and there would have been the end of the matter. But to run away, as if you had stolen some silver spoons—good Heavens, Loveday! Juliot and Paul will be imagining all sorts of things.'

'No, Constantine, there you are mistaken.'

'I am not mistaken. I am alarmed for myself. It is I am in danger, not you. You think only of how you may get away from a place where you have had a great shock and grief. I do not blame you for wishing to leave, but I do blame you greatly for putting me in danger. You should not be selfish, Loveday. Selfishness is objectionable in a man, but it is offensive in a woman.'

'What will you have me do, now?' asked Loveday, unwilling to argue.

'Do—there is nothing that can be done but remain where you are. You are like a draughtsman on a board driven into a corner, with only two moves, one forward and one back. Here you are safe enough, if you do not take flight again. Do you suppose that happiness is to be caught, as a child goes after a bird, with a pinch of salt to clap on its tail? Happiness will come to you in good time, if you take matters easy, and do not go racing over the country with your reticule in your hand, chasing it.'

'You quite mistake me,' said Loveday, gravely. 'I have given up all hopes of happiness. I left Marsland because I could not remain there after Mr. Featherstone had asked me to be his wife.'

'That was what Paul meant by taking you out in the boat, was it? Juliot played into his hands. A pair of ninnies, both.' Constantine

was angry. If he loved any one beside himself,
that person was Loveday. 'Nothing in the
world would give me greater pleasure than to
take a cudgel to his head and beat the nonsense out of it. Unfortunately, just now, and
till you are well away, I am in his power, and
he may do me a cursed turn—show me the
white horse, as the wrestlers say as they give
the fling that breaks the backbone. I wish it
were in my power to kick up his heels. I
shall have it some day. I must wait my time,
and then I shall pay him out for daring to insult you with his addresses.'

'You must not speak thus,' said Loveday.
'Mr. Featherstone is the soul of honour. If he
addressed me, he did so with respect, and in
ignorance of my position, which ignorance is
due to you, who dare not tell him the truth.'

'Oh, you reproach me!' said Constantine,
angrily. 'The compliment of an offer has disposed you to think kindly of the crackbrained
quack. You turn against me, of course, follow-
ing the rest. Such is the way of the world.
My father never had a good word for me, and
Gerans was the hero. I was always in the
background, always forced to play second fiddle.

Now, because I am in difficulty and danger, even you will not spare me.'

'Constantine!' She looked reproachfully at him, and he coloured.

'I meant no harm,' he said. 'You must make allowances for me. I am harassed and nervous. I live in daily terror of discovery. Perhaps you have not fully realised what discovery would entail on me.'

'What am I to do now? May I not go?'

'You must remain concealed in this place. On no account allow any one to see you. I have no doubt that that fool Featherstone will be stirring up the neighbourhood in quest of you. I have insisted on old Carwithen and his wife holding their tongues. None but they know that you are here. As soon as I can I will get you away by boat to Clovelly. Give me time to consider what is best, and all will come right. I'm like a boy with a puzzle map. It is confusion now, but with patience I shall make it out and fit all into a consistent whole. Now I'm poking the toe of Italy in the side of Russia, and fitting Timbuctoo into Great Britain.'

'I have no clothes fit to go in,' said Loveday. 'Everything is in my box at Marsland.'

'There it must remain. You must not meddle with that. I will see what I can get for you. Or, stay! write a letter as if from Exeter, and say you have found a home there with your cousin, and I will get it posted to Juliot.'

'No,' answered Loveday. 'I will not speak or write an untruth. I want to be somewhere whence I can write. I cannot remain here for long.'

'Stay a week. Only a week. Before seven days are past something shall be decided. Now I must go. Tamsin Carwithen must not see us so long together, or she will suspect something.'

CHAPTER XLVI.

RICHARD CARWITHEN.

LOVEDAY was not missed at first by Paul and Juliot. She did not appear at breakfast, but neither was surprised, because they thought she was tired with the excursion on the water, and hoped that she had overslept herself and was recruiting her strength.

'Well, Paul?' said Juliot, with inquiry in her tone and in the look of her eyes.

Paul Featherstone sighed, and shook his head. 'I was too precipitate, Juliot. I feared it myself, but you encouraged me. She has had great sorrows which have so crushed her that she cannot yet look up. She is like a bruised and broken flower, lying on the ground; we must raise her, and tie her up, and have patience, allow the sap to flow, and the healing processes to begin. We must not demand fresh bloom of the flower this season ; we must be satisfied if it does not wither away.'

'I thought that your regard, dear Paul, would have been the stay for the flower. It would have held to that and become strong.'

'Juliot, I have reproached myself severely for my haste. But I acted from the best motive. I desired to be honourable and open with her. As she was in the house, and had won my respect and love, I did not consider it proper to leave her in ignorance of my sentiments, and to allow her to settle into a house in a menial position when I purposed to make her its mistress. But I was too precipitate. I hurt and alarmed her.'

'Oh, Paul! what will she do now? She will hardly be induced to stay here if she has refused your addresses.'

Featherstone leaned back, and looked with dismay at his sister. 'Juliot!' he exclaimed, 'I had not thought of that. Where is Rock?'

'John went back to Stanbury last night. He is very busy there.'

'So it seems. He used not to be there so much. But the place has demands on him. Now he is there all day and night as well.'

'He tells me the men there need much supervision.'

Paul left Marsland after breakfast, without saying whither he was going, consequently he was not at home when the discovery was made that Loveday had fled. Her packed box, the bed not slept in, showed that she had gone. Juliot sent after her brother, but Paul was not to be found, and did not return till noon. Then, only, was he made aware of Loveday's disappearance.

The morning had been lost in looking for him. Juliot was incapable of giving directions for a search. Paul was filled with consternation and self-reproach. 'Oh, poor soul, poor soul!' he exclaimed, 'I have driven her from her newly discovered retreat. Juliot, she *must* be found and brought back; it is not she, it is I who must go. It is my fault that this has come about. I will go to Stanbury, and let Rock live here for a while. She must not be driven away. God be merciful to her! She is in no fit condition of mind or body for a journey.'

'Whither has she gone?' asked Juliot.

'I doubt not, towards Exeter,' answered Paul. 'She let fall, as I was driving her here, something about a cousin whom she had purposed visiting when arrested on her journey by my advertisement. She has certainly started on her way thither. I shall reproach myself for this all my days. The weather is changing. We shall have a storm this afternoon, and she may be exposed to it!' He ordered the horse to be put in the trap at once. There was room in this conveyance for two only. 'Juliot,' said Paul, 'I shall take Willy Penrose with me, and when we find her I shall alight and let Willy drive her home, and I will come after afoot.'

Paul spent the whole afternoon in the storm, driving from place to place making inquiries, always without result. The district was thinly populated, and there were more ways than one by which Loveday might have gone. No main road ran thence in the direction of Exeter, but lanes and parish roads led away, an intricate ramification, towards villages to the east. Had she gone across country by one of these towards Torrington? or had she gone by another to Holsworthy? or had she taken the main road along the coast to Hartland, intending to follow thence the highway to Exeter through Bideford? or had she gone along the coast to Stratton, to take the coach thence to Launceston? It was uncertain which of all these ways she had gone. One was just as near as another. There was actually only one direction in which she could not have gone—due west, over the cliffs, and into the sea.

Paul, disappointed on one road, took another; the horse became fagged, his companion dissatisfied. The storm raged about them. The rain drenched them, driving through all the clothes they wore, forming a pool in the bottom of the gig. Now and then the horse stood still, and obstinately refused to stir, till some whirling rush of rain had spent itself. The tempest defeated the object of Paul. It was most likely that Loveday had taken refuge somewhere off the road. It drove every one indoors, there was no traffic, therefore none to see her, if she did pass. Late in the evening, almost as wearied as his horse and man, but reluctant still to give up the search, Paul turned homewards : perhaps he would not have done that but for the hope that some tidings of the missing girl had been obtained nearer home—that, possibly, she might have been driven back by the storm. It was, to him, unaccountable that

no one had seen her, yet he had asked at every
cottage he had passed, of every traveller he had
encountered.

When he reached home, he was disappointed.
Nothing had been learned of her. The servants
were questioned. The only thing that could be
elicited from them was that the hall door was
discovered to be unlocked in the morning. Not
a line was found in her room to afford a clue.
There was no fresh direction on the box to
show whither it was to be sent. The old
address to her cousin's in Exeter was, indeed,
there, scored through with a pencil. On his
return Paul wrote at once to this address, but
too late for the post.

'Has Rock been here, Juliot?'

'No, Paul. I suppose the tempest has de-
tained him at Stanbury.'

'I have been everywhere but thither. It
is mysterious, prodigiously strange to me. She
seems to have disappeared as effectually as if
the earth had swallowed her up.'

'Take off your wet clothes, Paul, or you
will be laid up. You are not a strong man.
You must have a posset, and go to bed.'

'I—I take a hot posset!' exclaimed Paul,

'and she—she, poor soul, whom I drove from this house by my persecution is, perhaps, in cold, and wet, and hunger! My God! I cannot bear to think of what may be! Oh, Juliot, Juliot!' He was overcome with emotion. He took his sister by the hand, and covered his face with the other.

'I'll get a change of clothes,' he said, when he had recovered himself; 'but I cannot go to bed. I have sent Will Penrose home, he is tired and wet and out of temper; and I have bid Roger Gale harness the other horse and bring him round in half an hour.'

'But night is set in; whither are you going?'

'I shall drive now to Stratton. I have thought that she may have avoided the nearest houses and made for the town; we came thence, and she would naturally think to go back thither. There she knows a coach is to be caught which would carry her away. I will drive to-night to Stratton, and make inquiries. She may even have gone thither by the coast through Stanbury. Rock might give us news if he were here, but I doubt her having gone that way; she would have passed Stanbury before the storm broke, and Rock would for certain have brought her back. It is much more likely that she would go by the way she came, and avoid the houses.'

Then he went to his room and changed his clothes. When vested in a dry suit he came down, and hastily took some refreshment. 'I will go alone now,' said he; 'I will not take Roger with me. Even if I found her, I would not bring her home to-night, but place her where she would be safe and well cared for.'

Then he departed. The storm was over, the violence of the gale had spent itself, but it left behind a small drizzle that in time would wet one exposed to it as thoroughly as the previous pelting rain.

It was late at night, or rather very early in the morning, when Paul returned. His journey had been in vain. He had been to every inn in the little town of Stratton, but could hear nothing of Loveday. He left word at the coach office that she was not to go till he had been communicated with, should she appear there. And, finally, he announced at each of the inns that he would give a liberal golden reward to any one who should bring him information which might lead to her recovery.

When Paul Featherstone came home he was completely worn out in body and in mind. He was not a strong man, and the exposure to the wet and the wind for twelve hours, and the strain on his nerves, had exhausted him. He threw off his sodden garments, and went to bed, but he could not sleep. He could think only of the poor girl, a wanderer, in the storm, without a home to which to go, without a friend on whom to lean. She was not restored to her full strength since her illness. Had she succumbed? Was she lying dead behind a hedge, or in a copse? His brow was as wet, and not his brow only, his eyes as well, at the thought, as if they were still in the drift of the rain. He put both his hands over his face, and as he lay, hour by hour, instead of thinking further of what might have happened, he prayed.

Next morning Constantine appeared.

'Well, Featherstone! how are you all after the storm? The wind took our new hayrick and blew it over. To-day, if middling fine, we shall try to dry the hay, and rick it again. Was your hay thatched? We didn't reckon on such a gale, did we?'

Then Paul told him of the loss of Loveday.

'Don't you trouble your head about her,' said Constantine, with affected composure. 'The poor creature was evidently off her head, and has gone over the cliffs into the sea. I never supposed her right in the brain—gone melancholy mad. I've heard of such cases.'

Paul looked at him with horror. The idea that Loveday had come to an end in this way had not occurred to him. Even now he could hardly bring himself to entertain the conjecture that she had voluntarily destroyed herself, but he remembered that she had walked in her sleep once, and it was possible that she had again gone sleep-walking in the direction of the sea. No doubt but her thoughts that night had been on the excursion with him in the boat; what more likely than that she had dreamt of the sea, and gone towards it— perhaps down the same road they had traversed together, to and from the bay?

This thought made such an impression on Paul that he left the house immediately, and descended the lane to Marsland Mouth, and there searched the beach. Not a trace of Loveday was to be found. He went to the

boathouse and searched that. He explored
the caves in the rocks. Nowhere a token that
she had been there—the tide had risen and
ebbed since they had left the boat, so that
every foot-mark on the sand was effaced.

When slowly and sadly, and, it must be
added, wearily, he ascended the steep hill to
Marsland, his attention was caught by the
bush of ash from which he had cut the staff
for Loveday. Where was that staff? He
considered when he reached home. The staff
was gone. She must have taken it with her.
Surely, then, she intended it for a support on
a long or steep walk. This and the packed
box, and the unslept-in bed, satisfied him that
she had not gone from the house walking in
her sleep. That she had taken the stick with
her assured him that she had not meditated
suicide.

It was a relief to him to think this. It
was a comfort to him, a very minute one, but
still something of a comfort, to think that the
staff he had cut for her had been a stay to her.

Three days passed, and still no news of
Loveday. The anxiety was wearing Paul, who
reproached himself, unnecessarily and un-

reasonably, but he had an over-sensitive conscience. His fears that she might have been
overcome by exhaustion, and died in the
storm, or that in the cloud and driving rain
she might have fallen over the cliffs, returned.
He went in a boat along the coast, searching
every margin of sand, but still, ineffectually.
He went round the neighbourhood again, offer-
ing rewards, but no one put in a claim for any.
He could attend to none of the business of the
farm. His mind was engrossed with the search
for Loveday.

'Please, your honour,' said Carwithen,
appearing before him as he went out on foot
down the avenue to resume his inquiries—he
had worn out his horses, and was obliged on
this day to give them rest—' please, your
honour,' said Carwithen, ' Scripture says, Thou
shalt not muzzle the ox that treadeth out the
corn. If you want to find the young lady,
you must pay folks for the trouble they take
in hunting after her.'

'I am ready to do so. Dick, have you
news? Do not keep what you may chance to
know from me. What has brought you from
Stanbury ? '

'Your honour, I thought I'd take the liberty of asking, How much?'

'What do you mean?'

'Your honour have promised a reward to such as can give information respecting Miss Penhalligan.'

'Dick Carwithen,' exclaimed Paul, suddenly, 'where did you find that staff of ash? I recognise it. I cut it for her the evening before she disappeared.'

'That may be. And it may be also that I can tell more than about where the stick were found. The truth of the matter is this, master. Squire Rock and I don't hit it off together as I should like. Scripture says, Thou shalt not plough with an ox and an ass together.'

'Tell me,' said Featherstone, 'tell me straight out, what you have discovered. I will reward you.'

'Look here, master, it turns to this, How much? Just as all men turn to dust and ashes, so do all questions turn to guineas and shillings. What will you pay?'

'Name your price,' said Paul, impatiently.

'There's that little holding of forty acres at Coombe,' said Carwithen. 'Old Kennard is dying, and when he's gone it will be vacant : he had it for life, as he reclaimed it out of the moor. Now, if I may have that at three shillings an acre for fourteen years' lease I'll tell you a good deal.'

Paul looked at him with surprise and disgust.

'Ah!' said Carwithen, 'I'll do more than tell you, I'll take you where you shall see her, but whether alive or dead I won't say till you give me my price. If I tread out your corn, I mustn't be muzzled. Let me assure you of this—if you don't hear it from me you will never know anything more about her.'

Paul gave way at once.

'Come with me down to Marsland Mouth,' said Carwithen, 'and we will go by boat under the rocks.' Then he laughed. 'I was not to have a hind's place any longer, but to be reduced to work as a labourer and have a labourer's wage!'

CHAPTER XLVII.

DISCOVERED.

CONSTANTINE went every day to Featherstone's
Kitchen, especially at such times as he knew
Tamsin Carwithen would not be there. Tamsin
came to the house at Stanbury daily to assist
her mother with the washing ; and Constantine
took the occasion for slipping off to the Kitchen
on the cliff, so as to enjoy a long conversation
with Loveday unobserved.

The old inclination for Loveday revived in
his heart, and the attraction that drew him
to her originally again exerted over him its
former power. The notice that Paul took of
her had made him jealous, and he was angry
with him for having dared to propose to her.
A first love is always surrounded with a halo
of romance which surrounds no second love.
Moreover, Constantine had never really cared

for Juliot. He had taken her for the sake of
Stanbury and an easy life. He was tired of
the monotony of his existence at Marsland,
impatient of the fear which kept him there a
prisoner, and, when he saw Loveday again, he
longed to recover what he had lost or thrown
away. The recollection—the old courtship,
the early happy love—spun its delicate gleaming magic fibres round his heart, and filled
him with melancholy. How happy he would
have been with her, if he had had the courage
to confess his marriage to the old Squire, and
his father had accepted it, and made him a
small allowance, which, with what he earned
in an office, would have sufficed to support
them! What might have been is always so
superior to what is.

He had forfeited Loveday's regard, but
hardly lost her love. Was it wholly impossible
for him to recover the regard?

Surely not, if he showed her good proof of
repentance.

He was uneasy at the efforts made by Paul
Featherstone to find her. Wherever he went,
he heard nothing talked about but the missing
lady. The labourers leaned on their picks and

discussed the subject. He was asked by every
one he met whether any news about her had
reached Marsland. Carwithen took a grim
delight in exciting his alarm. What the relation was between Mr. Rock and the lady
Richard Carwithen could not understand, nor
why his master pressed him with such urgency
to be silent. Constantine had no fear of Carwithen betraying him, because he supposed it
was the old man's interest to remain in favour
with him, as Squire of Stanbury, and because
Carwithen, he knew, had no regard for Paul
Featherstone. He had, moreover, promised to
pay him the same reward for keeping the secret
as Featherstone had offered for news of the
lost lady.

'I can get no sleep,' said Constantine to
Loveday. 'Paul is raising an insane hue-and-
cry, and disturbing the entire country. I
want your bonnet and cloak. I will throw them
into the sea ; they will be washed ashore, and
then, perhaps, this prodigious fuss will abate—
Paul will suppose that you have drowned yourself.'

'I will not let you have them for this
purpose,' answered Loveday. 'I would not

have Mr. Featherstone suppose it of me, that I
could destroy myself.'

'Oh! he may think you tumbled over the
cliffs, and were drowned accidentally.'

Loveday made no reply to this, and Constantine, seeing he had annoyed her, did not
press the point.

'I am much afraid,' she said, after a while,
'that my brother will be alarmed as well, and
make inquiries all the way from Wadebridge to
Launceston, and so be led on to Marsland; then
all will come out.'

Constantine turned livid. He had not considered this danger.

'Loveday,' he said, after a few moments of
anxious thought, as he paced the turf near the
cottage, 'I have made up my mind; I will do
what you advised. I will leave Marsland for
ever, Marsland and Stanbury both. I will go
out into the world, and begin life afresh. I
have acted very wrongly, and I will use my
best endeavour to undo the wrong. I tell you,
Loveday, that I cannot bear myself for my
error, and I am terribly scared at the prospect
that it entails. I can have no peace any more,
now that I have seen you again. After all—

you are my wife—my own dear wife, to whom
I am bound, with whom I promised to fight
through the world. I tell you the whole truth,
Loveday, I have never, never loved any one but
you. You I loved in the dear, happy old days
at Towan, days of innocence and brightness. I
lie awake at night and think of them. Whilst
I am about the farm all day I am recalling
them. I did wrong in not telling my father at
once when we married. I did wrong in persuading you to marry me without asking his
consent. One wrong act, we are told, draws on
a chain of others. It has been so in this case,
I have proved it; and I reproach myself for the
first and all that followed. But I suppose it is
inevitable. If once we do wrong, we must go on
from wrong to wrong till brought to our senses.
That, I presume, is a moral necessity, a law of
the universe, just like gravitation, and the revo-
lution of the sun. Now I see what I have done,
and am resolved never to do anything that is
wrong again. I loved you always, and I will
love you ever, as I promised and vowed, and if
you have the spirit of Christianity in you, you
will forgive me.'

When Constantine told Loveday that he

loved her, and her only, then, as was natural, her heart bounded and her cheeks flushed. But the excitation was momentary, the colour went again, and her pulse resumed its ordinary beat. She shook her head. She tried to speak, but her words failed.

'I will tell you what my plan is,' continued Constantine. 'I have resolved to leave England. I cannot settle anywhere in the British Isles. If that owl, Paul, makes such a disturbance because you are lost, who are nothing to him, what a tenfold disturbance will he make to find me, whom he married to his sister. He would stir up the whole country till I was tracked out. No, no, Loveday. That will never do for me. I will leave the country. I will go to America, where, in a new world, I may begin a new and a better life—with you.'

Loveday had been seated. She started to her feet and walked abruptly away, along the down, to be for a few moments by herself to consider this proposal of Constantine's. She was his wife. It was her duty to be with him. He loved her and loved her only. She loved him and him only. He had sinned against her and against Juliot. Ought she so far to forget the past as to accompany him? She could not answer this question at once. Indeed she hardly put it to herself as a question to be decided at once. She was overcome by the offer, by the glimmer it afforded her of a future home.

Constantine lacked the tact to leave her to herself. He went after her. He went from the extreme of despondency to the most sanguine elation. His scheme was perfect. All would come right now. He was learned in the law—that is, he had been a few years in an office, engrossing—and would be certain to obtain a judgeship in the United States. He was perfectly acquainted with the management of a farm. He would obtain a grant of land, and build a log-house, and Loveday and he would dwell together in it, as happy as two wood-pigeons. He was well-educated, he would set up a school and charge high, and train young American citizens in knowledge and virtue, and realise a fortune—a man of parts from England could not fail to succeed. Anything, everything was open to him.

'Oh, Constantine!' exclaimed Loveday, 'what would Mr. Featherstone and Juliot think if they found that we had gone together to America? I would not that she should know how she has been deceived by you, and I would not have him think unworthily of me.'

'What can it matter what their opinion is of us, when we are beyond the sea? Besides, I would write to Featherstone and tell him everything. Then the responsibility of un-deceiving his sister would lie on his shoulders, and he would not think ill of you. He would, on the contrary, think highly of you for follow-ing your proper husband over the Atlantic to his new home.'

'Oh, Constantine!' said she, in a tone of agony, distressed by the conflicting feelings in her bosom, 'is it really, really true that you love me alone, that you will forget poor Juliot and the little child she has borne to you?'

'If it were not so, would I make this pro-posal to you?' he answered. 'Consider the sacrifice I am ready to make at the altar of duty. I lose Stanbury, a comfortable home, and a nice fortune, to go forth in poverty, as an exile—what for? Because, Loveday, my conscience tells me I ought to do it. When conscience speaks we must obey. And in this case inclination jumps with obligation. I have told you I love you. I cannot live away from you. If you refuse to come with me I will stay in England, but I will not remain here with Juliot. I will follow you wherever you go; I will follow you like a dog. You shall not be able to shake me off, except in one way, by delivering me over to justice; and that you will not do—you are too noble, too generous, too good at heart. That is a contingency not to be considered. Remember that you are my wife in the sight of heaven, that you are responsible to heaven for me. If you let me go alone to America, I do not know what will become of me. I shall have nothing to live for—no home, no happiness. I dare say I shall take to drink and perish miserably. Of course you will come with me. You are not, I trust, lost to all sense of religion and moral obligation.'

Loveday musing looked into his face, and shook her head, whilst pressing her hands on her heaving bosom. Could she flatter herself that her reappearance had driven Juliot wholly from his heart? That in a foreign land the yearning for his little son would not awake in him and make him restless to return to England and see his child again? Was he one who would endure the privations of exile? One who had sufficient tenacity of purpose to hold to his resolution? In America, if they had to undergo hardships, would he not turn against her, and reproach her with banishment? Was he trustworthy? Also, she felt great repugnance against uniting her lot with him now, after his treachery and falsehood, and the wrong he had done to her and to Juliot and to Paul.

' I love you,' she said, ' I love you dearly. God, who reads the heart, knows it. But what happiness would I find if I knew you were unhappy? I am glad that you still love me ; but we can never be happy together again—never ! '

'My dear Loveday,' exclaimed Constantine, ' what nonsense you talk ! Of course we can be happy together. In a new world, amid fresh scenes, fresh occupations, surrounded by new people, we shall be quite happy. We shall shake off all these unpleasantnesses, like a dog who gets out of a bath. He shakes himself, and away fly the drops in all direc-

tions, and in ten minutes he is dry as Paul
Featherstone. We shall sit together over our
own fireside and not give even a thought to the
past. Oh, Loveday, how happy we shall be !
Cares, fears, troubles drowned like Pharaoh in
the deep of the sea, sunk deeper than he, as the
Atlantic is more profound than the Red Sea.
We will have a garden of our own, and
put mignonette under the window—I am so
fond of the scent of mignonette—and we will
have a little summer-house in the corner of our
garden with Banksia roses trained over it;
that will be charming. And then we will sit
there in the evenings, and I will read to you
" Guy Mannering," whilst you knit my stockings. Have you read that? It is prodigiously
interesting. Then, consider this, my sweet
wife, we shall be in a climate that is dry.
Here we are in a warm bath and a steam alike
in every season. In America when the winter
sets in there is real cold weather, and in the
summer there is real heat. On my word,
Loveday, I am all eagerness to start.'

' Constantine,' said Loveday, looking at
him with eyes that streamed with tears, ' do
not try me with such pictures. It cannot be,

at least not now. That you should go is right,
and I do not say that after a time I will not
rejoin you, but not now, certainly not now.
Go yourself, and, if you think proper, write to
Mr. Featherstone and tell him the whole truth.
But I cannot go with you. Perhaps after
three years, when you have shown yourself in
earnest, I may follow, but I will not, I cannot,
go with you now. The sooner you go, the
better. Do not delay; it is right that you
should depart.'

'This is unkind,' said Constantine, impatiently. 'You want to drive me away, and
you will not help me in my difficulties. It is
easy to say Go, but harder to do it. I have
little money, and one cannot cross the ocean
without means. I shall have to sell stock off
the farm, and raise something in spite of Paul
Featherstone, who will ask me what I am
about.'

'If you have no right to make money on
Stanbury, do not try to do it. Take my advice
once again, Constantine. Be straightforward
and truthful. Go, as the prodigal in the parable, and your father will not cast you out. Confess everything to Mr. Gaverock and ask him to

help you to cross to America. He will certainly assist you, and assist you liberally. Is he not your father? Then from Towan write to Mr. Featherstone, and tell him the whole truth, and tell him you are leaving England for ever, a penitent for the wrong you have done. He is so good, he will accept your repentance, and not attempt pursuit and demand chastisement. You must write, leaving all to him. If he were to demand your punishment, accept it; give him the time to decide whether he will punish, or whether he will pardon. That will be most honourable, and when he has granted you leave to depart unmolested, go. After three years, Constantine, when you have proved your own heart, if you still desire my presence, I will cross the ocean to you, and I will never by word or look reproach you for the past, but freely, heartily forgive you your trespass against me, as I look for forgiveness of my trespasses from heaven. There, Constantine, in pledge of my sincerity I give you my hand—no—not one, I give you both.'

As she held out her arms, and he clasped her hands, they were startled by the appearance of Paul Featherstone, standing before

them. Their backs had been turned to the
path that ascended the cliff from the little
strand, but as she gave Constantine her hands
she turned, intending to go back to the cottage,
having said her last words. In so turning she
saw Paul, and her start induced Constantine to
turn also. Constantine turned pale with fear,
and dropped the hands of Loveday. She felt
the blood rush to her face and temples. She
covered her eyes with her hands, and fled to
the hovel.

CHAPTER XLVIII.

A STROKE.

PAUL FEATHERSTONE and Constantine Gaverock stood confronting each other. Both were pale as chalk.

Constantine was in deadly fear lest Paul should have heard any portion of his conversation with Loveday. But Paul had not caught a word. He could not have approached to listen to them ; to do this was repugnant to his character. But he had seen enough to send the blood to his heart. She whom he had been seeking everywhere was living concealed under the protection of his brother-in-law. She had run away from Marsland to be near him. That they were on very intimate terms their conversation, and the way in which they had held each other's hands, the dismay with which they had started asunder on seeing him, sufficiently

proved. He had been hurt by the coldness
and callousness of Rock towards the suffering
girl. It had never occurred to him that this
might be assumed to disguise a warmer feeling.
Now he was too startled to consider the relation
in which they stood to each other, or account
for the intimacy, to speculate when it had be-
gun, and to what an extent it had been carried.

Constantine was the first to recover his self-
possession sufficiently to ask Paul what he
wanted there. Had he come in quest of him?

Paul Featherstone turned his eyes slowly
upon him. He had been looking after Loveday, flying to the cottage. He was over-
whelmed by the double betrayal of himself and
his sister.

'I do not seek you,' answered he, gravely.
'Not you—certainly not you—the husband of
my sister Juliot.'

Constantine winced; but the words of Paul
afforded him some relief. Paul would not have
emphasised the relationship if he had any sus-
picions of the truth. This conviction revived
his courage.

'What do you want?' he asked. 'I know
you have extraordinary ways. Are you quali-

fying to act as Jack-in-the-box, popping up
unexpectedly under one's nose?'

Featherstone did not deign a reply; he had
a dark vein on his brow, and this swelled.
When he was much disturbed it puffed and
became purple. He was indignant and angry,
but he had not lost his usual self-control, his
somewhat pedantic stateliness of manner.

'There is nothing wonderful in a poor girl
seeking protection with me against your impertinence,' said Constantine. He stooped,
picked a pink-flowering thrift, and began to
bite the stalk. His jaws were trembling; he
did this to conceal the chatter of his teeth.
'Do you not think,' asked Constantine, with
low cunning, attacking his brother-in-law to
protect himself from assault, 'do you not think
that the advertisement in "The Light of the
West" was worded wrong, and should have
stood, " Wanted, a companion for Paul Featherstone; young, pretty, and sanctimonious"?'

'Rock!' said Paul, sternly, 'be silent.'

'I have a duty to perform,' said Constantine, defiant in self-defence. 'When a young
lady whom you have beguiled into your house
is driven by your insolent addresses to escape

from it; when she flies to me—a married man
—to protect her; throws herself upon my
honour and chivalry to ward off your offensive
persecutions, then I am only doing my duty as
a gentleman when I say to you, Go back the
way you came, and trouble her no more.
Good Heavens! the whole country is ringing
with your scandalous conduct; your name is
coupled with hers in a way intolerable to the
modesty of a virtuous gentlewoman. Every
one laughs and winks, and says an aside behind
his hand, when you pass along the road nose in
air, hunting the pretty and pious companion.'

'Rock!' exclaimed Paul, his eyes flashing
with indignation.

'It is very sanctimonious for you to profess
to be shocked when I tell you the truth. You
have hoodwinked yourself as well as others.
You live in a world of self-delusion, and it is
well that I can pluck you out of it and show
you the contemptible figure you make, as
viewed from outside. In a fog a sheep is mag-
nified to the size of an elephant, and in the fog
you live in nothing bears its proper proportions.
You had the temerity, when Miss Penhalligan
was ill, to force yourself into her room, and

make your passes over her face, and press her
hand under the pretence of feeling her pulse.
When she recovers you take her out on the
water, and make a point of rowing behind the
rocks where you may be out of sight, and you
take the base advantage of being alone with
her in a boat, when you know she is unable to
escape, and I am not at hand to protect her, to
pester her with vulgar and insolent attentions.
Bah! Whether you be most fool or rogue I
do not pretend to say. I should be sorry to
make the analysis of such nasty material. A
little of all sorts, made up as a Chinaman
makes a picture of a plant with the flower of
one stock on the stalk of another, garnished
with the leaves of a third.'

'You despicable fellow,' said Paul, with his
black brows knit and his eyes flashing wrath-
fully. 'You are not worthy to be answered
by a man of honour. I am ready enough to
allow that I am full of fault, and may, unknown to myself, have fallen into follies and
error; but I know you now out of your own
mouth, the outpouring of your base mind, I
know you. I have long dreaded the discovery,
and have shrunk from it; now you stand

revealed to me in all your vileness. Had
I known what a dishonourable, ill-disposed
creature you were, I would have struck you
with the marlingspike when you clung to the
side of my boat, and not have held out a hand
to save you. Or, had I saved your life, as I
might have that of a dog, I would never have
admitted you under my roof, to bring on it
grief, and shame, and dishonour.'

Constantine flamed up with rage. He
could cast insults at another, but could not
endure to hear the truth spoken of himself.

'Cursed be the day,' he exclaimed, 'that
ever I came under that roof of yours, that ever
I crossed your threshold. From that day I date
all my misery. You—you and your sister
have made me what I am, an unhappy, tor-
mented man.'

These words of Constantine confirmed the
suspicion of Paul. They were the confession
of his love for Loveday, and his alienation from
Juliot, his wife. Exasperated to the last degree
by this infidelity towards his sister, he uttered
a groan of wrath and pain, and raised the ash
staff he held, and thrust with it at his brother-
in-law, to repel him. The action was hasty ;

he did not intend to strike him, but to express his horror. The touch of the stick was sufficient to make Constantine blind with fury. He shook Featherstone off, wrenched the staff from his grasp, and struck him with it a blow so violent that Paul staggered back and fell against a stone. He tried to gather himself up ; he was deadly pale. A stream of blood poured from his head. He swayed on his knees, put forth his hands to find support, and sank back on the turf.

Then Constantine heard a cry—and in another moment Loveday flew past him, knelt on the ground, and raised Paul in her arms, and strove to staunch his blood with her kerchief.

Constantine stood staring at Paul's white face, and the streaming blood, without stirring, without thinking, frozen with consternation at what he had done.

His rage evaporated, and his fears gained the upper hand. He looked about him. No one was present. None had seen the struggle save Loveday.

Now all was over. The secret must come out. It could be retained no longer. This quarrel with Paul would inevitably lead to his detection.

'What have you done?' cried Loveday. 'Oh, Con! Con! You have killed him, and added one sin to another. Run! Bring me water! Help me to carry him to the house! Oh, Con! I would you had struck and killed me instead.'

Constantine ran to the edge of the cliff, then returned.

'Loveday,' said he, 'there is the boat below in which Paul Featherstone came. I shall take it and be off. I cannot, I dare not remain. Come with me. It will be safer for me if you do; then nothing can be extracted from you to criminate me.'

'Oh, Constantine, run for water! I cannot leave him in this condition, insensible.'

'Let him be—he is not killed, he is hurt, that is all, and when he comes round can practise passes on himself. It will be an occupation and an amusement. Come along, Loveday! No time is to be lost. The weather is fine, and I will row down the coast till we reach Towan; then we will go together before my father, and ask his forgiveness and favour.'

'I cannot go with you; I have told you that I will not do so. Now, least of all, when Mr. Featherstone is in this condition. Bring me water.'

'How selfish you are, Loveday, you do not think of me. I must get away. I entreat you —as your husband I command you—to accompany me.'

'Constantine, you have forfeited your right to command. When you have recovered my respect again I will submit to your orders, not earlier.'

'There! he is becoming conscious. Come, or I shall believe that you care more for Paul Featherstone than for me.'

'Constantine!' she looked at him with an indignant flash in her dark eyes.

'I am not going to wait and waste valuable time,' said he. 'If you will not come, stay and coddle Paul Featherstone. It will be some time before I send for a disobedient wife.'

Without looking at her again he descended the path to the beach. Carwithen, seeing him, hid behind a rock, fearing his anger. But

Constantine had not observed him. He went to the boat, jumped in, and rowed himself away.

'Towan!' he said, 'yes, that is my only chance now. I will return to Towan.'

CHAPTER XLIX.

THE LAST CORD.

CARWITHEN came up the path in the face of the cliff after Constantine had gone off with the boat. On seeing that Paul Featherstone was hurt, and resting in Loveday's arms, he came to his assistance. Shortly after Thomasine also arrived, and Paul was brought to consciousness, and was sufficiently recovered to stand. He had received a cut in the back of his head, and had lost a good deal of blood, but there was nothing dangerous in the wound—the skull was not broken.

Loveday had taken the white kerchief from her neck and bound it round his head tightly, and arrested the bleeding.

He signed to Carwithen and his daughter to withdraw, and then he said to Loveday: 'Madam, I shall feel obliged if you will say nothing about a struggle with Mr. Rock. The cut in my head was made by a stone in the ground, against which I fell.'

Loveday bowed her consent. There was an expression of sadness in his eyes as he looked at her that went to her heart.

'Mr. Featherstone,' she said, timidly, 'I pray you not to judge me by appearances. I pray you to be pitiful and forbearing.'

'Madam,' he said, but he paused a long time before he spoke, 'He who is over all knows how anxious, how eager I am to excuse you, but I cannot condone what is unexplained.'

She was silent. He waited for her to speak, but as she said nothing he went on slowly, sadly—'I will go in now to the cottage. Carwithen will attend to me. He can manage so trifling a cut as that I have received. I will return presently, and listen with patience to what you may wish to say, in the hope that you will be able to relieve my mind of a great —— pain.' Then he withdrew.

Loveday was left alone. Her shoulders and neck were uncovered, she had torn off her kerchief for Paul's head. His blood stained the bosom of her gown. There was a little water near the cottage—a land spring, and she washed it thereat. Then she stood on the cliff looking seaward. She saw Constantine's boat, but he was already so far off that she could not distinguish him. She thought over what had taken place, and considered what she could say to Mr. Featherstone—how she could give a colourable explanation of her conduct. She could not account for her presence there satisfactorily. Would he believe that she had found her way to Stanbury by accident? If he were persuaded that this was so, how could she explain the intimacy with Constantine? She saw that to exculpate herself she must betray him, and, however unworthy he might be, that she could not do. If she had any lingering regard for Constantine after the discovery of his falsehood, he had dispelled it now by his insolence and injustice to Paul Featherstone. For this latter, Loveday had conceived the deepest respect. His simplicity of character, his earnest desire to do what was right and kind, had touched her heart; and the ungenerosity, the ingratitude of Constantine in attacking him, had filled her with horror and repugnance. She had known him to be weak; she now saw his irremediable worthlessness. If he had had any spark of good feeling lingering in his heart he could not have taunted Paul with such words. He was a coward and a scoundrel.

With this discovery her love for him died, as her respect had died. Now he had dragged her into the lowest humiliation. He had left her to bear the shame of being regarded by Paul Featherstone as a woman lost to gratitude and to honour. Rather than that she should be lightly thought of, Constantine would have braved the worst had he possessed a manly spirit. He had preferred to expose her to shame, and escape himself from danger.

In about a quarter of an hour Paul Featherstone came forth from the cottage. Richard Carwithen had patched up the wound in his head with plaster, of which he fortunately had some. Paul came forward to Loveday, who was sitting meditatively on a sand-hill. She rose as he approached. He was very pale—paler than could be accounted for by the amount of blood he had lost.

'Will you permit me,' he said, 'to ask you a few questions, madam?'

She had noticed that he ceased to address

her as *Miss* Penhalligan after he had learned
that she was a widow.   She bowed her head.

'You will allow me to lean on this staff?'
he said, kneeling and picking up that with
which Constantine had struck him.   'I am
shaken by the blow, and shall be glad of the
support.'

He shrank from putting the questions to her
which he had to put to her.

'I have thought it advisable to ask you a
few things—to—to save you much speaking.
It will be simpler and better.   Carwithen has
told me that Mr. Rock is gone.   He took the
boat and rowed away in the direction of Bude,
not towards Marsland.'

'Mr. Featherstone,' said Loveday, in a low
tone, with her hands clasped before her and
her eyes on the ground, 'I may tell you this—
he is gone for ever.   You will see him no
more.'

Then she was silent; and he did not speak,
but she felt that his eyes were on her face,
searching it.

'Why has he gone?'

She was unable to answer.

'Madam,' he said, in a very low tone, and

his voice shook as he spoke, 'as I was returning to consciousness I thought I heard his voice addressing you, and asking you to accompany him. And—I heard you refuse?'

'Yes.' She was as white as himself, and she was trembling.

He clutched the staff, but his fingers opened and closed and worked nervously on it.

'I would say——enough,' he continued, after a long pause, 'but that I *must* know something more. I have my sister, my dear sister, to consider.' Then he stopped. He was not strong enough, after the blow and fall and the loss of blood, to proceed rapidly, and every sentence was torn from him with a wrench of pain.

'I would hear further. Did you know him? Was there any attachment to—to him before you came to Marsland?'

'Yes,' very faintly.

'One question more. Is Penhalligan your real name?'

'No.'

Then, involuntarily, a groan escaped him. Loveday looked up with terror. Had he divined the truth? No, he had not.

'Then,' he said slowly, articulating each

word distinctly, and each as it issued from his heart cost him a pang, and each as it fell on her ear entered and pierced her brain, 'under a feigned name you made your way into my home, you followed him whom you loved, and who, I suppose, loved you. And then, when he had arranged all, you fled to him, to Stanbury.'

With a cry of despair, putting up her quivering hands, she said, 'No! no!'

'Do not deny it,' he went on, mastering his emotion with an effort which covered his brow with sweat drops. 'You left Marsland, and came direct to Stanbury, where he was awaiting you. Carwithen told me all.'

What would her denial profit her? She raised her hands in speechless agony, put her fingers to her teeth, then let her hands fall again flat on her lap, and her head hung down on her bosom, as if it were a flower-head that had been struck and broken, but not broken off.

'And yet,' said he, 'I have to acknowledge a debt to you. The evening before you departed you behaved honourably to me. When I asked you——'

She raised her hand to stop the words; she could not lift her eyes.

'You dealt with me conscientiously; you refused me. I thank God for that! both because it saved me from a terrible awakening when too late, but also for your own sake, because it shows me that your soul still stirs in response to generous feelings. And again, now, when he asked you to escape with him, the grace of God prevailed : you resisted the voice of the tempter, and——' He could not speak any more. He shook ; he was weeping ; he was enfeebled by what he had undergone, and unable at this moment to retain the mastery over himself.

At the sound of his broken voice, and the sob that issued from his heart, Loveday's frozen horror and despair gave way. She had been standing. She threw herself before him on her knees, she held up her clasped hands above her head, the tears poured from her eyes, and a storm of passionate weeping choked her words.

'Have patience with me!—Have pity on me!—Do not condemn me!—Oh, do not think so badly of me!—I am not wicked!—I have been weak and have erred!—I beseech you pardon me!—It is not all as you say!—I am not so lost as that!—And you! you! you to cast me out!—You to scorn and reject me!' Then she bowed her face to the coarse sea-grass, and the pink and silver thrift, and the purple sea-lavender; and held her hands with the fingers interlaced tight, as though woven out of wire, over her lips to restrain them from saying more.

'I do not condemn you,' said Paul, calmly. He had recovered his composure, which had left him only for a moment. 'I should indeed be an unworthy servant of Him who stooped and wrote on the sand when such an other was brought before him if I did not pity with an infinite and loving pity instead of condemnation. Far from speaking words of condemnation, I am thanking heaven that you are repentant, and hoping that this is the beginning of a new life. Stand up, I pray you. Do not lie there in the sand. Be composed. We must consider the future.'

She obeyed him mechanically.

He walked away, leaning heavily on the staff, towards the edge of the cliff, and held his hand over his eyes, whilst he looked along the coast towards the south, as trying to see the boat in which Constantine was departing. He stood thus gazing for a long while motionless, but he saw nothing. It may be doubted whether he were in reality straining his eyes to follow the boat and find the direction it was taking. After some time, during which he stood motionless, with his back towards Loveday, he turned and came to her.

'Let us sit down,' he said, with composed voice. 'I am not strong enough to stand long just now. I can speak better, and with less effort, if you will allow me to take my place on this stone.' He did not look at her, fearing lest he should lose control over his voice if he saw her white tear-stained face, and large, entreating, anguish-brimming eyes.

'Madam,' he said, 'between you and me let the past be no more mentioned, or let it be spoken of as little as may be. I shall have to consider my sister, and break to her the news that she has lost her husband. I would spare her unnecessary pain; I would spare her the thought of evil. She must not hear your name associated with that of John Rock, she must have no suspicion that your disappearance is in any way mixed up with his departure. I trust you will suffer me to decide for you what is best. What is best for you is also best for us. You will allow me to rule your course for a little while?'

She bowed for an answer. He did not look at her, but he saw her shadow, and the motion of the shadow assured him of her consent.

'It will be advisable for you to remain here with Tamsin Carwithen, at least for a time.'

She assented, as before.

'You were taken in the storm, drenched to the skin, and were found in a state of exhaustion and unconsciousness by Carwithen, who brought you here. This is what I shall tell Juliot, and what shall be given to the world. It will suffice. Mr. Rock has gone away on business of his own. Has he gone to his home?'

Loveday hesitated to admit this.

'I have never asked him about his home. I understood he had none, and that his past was associated with misfortune. I did not press to know. I saw no need. Now I suspect that I was deceived by his very reticence. If you do not assure me to the contrary, I will assert that he has gone to his home on business of his own.'

Loveday offered no denial.

'What is to follow time will decide. It is

very important, madam, for your honour, that
you should remain here, and that it be known
throughout the neighbourhood that you are
here, and that here you should continue for
some time after it has become certain that
John Rock has departed, never to return.
You can understand my motives. I shall be
glad that you accept my decision for your own
sake, and for that of my sister.'

' It shall be so,' said Loveday.

' That you cannot return to Marsland, you
see for yourself. Should Juliot come to you
and entreat you to return, you must refuse.
You can say, what is true, that your health
incapacitates you from being of assistance
to her. You can be understood to reside
here, to lodge in this cottage with Tamsin
Carwithen, till your health is recruited. And
now, madam, farewell—for ever. I do not
suppose we shall meet again. It is best
not.' He stood up. ' Your box, left at Marsland, shall be sent to you here. I believe
the arrangement made—or contemplated—was
such that a half-yearly notice should be given,
and the salary was fixed, though not named.
You will allow me to send you what we *owe*

you; the notice to leave comes from me. Excuse me entering on these matters now, but, as I may not see you again, I desire to make everything clear. Your box shall be sent over to-day, and with it the sum of money to which you are entitled, together with a little present which you will not, I am sure, pain my sister by refusing.'

'Oh, Mr. Featherstone!' cried Loveday, 'Mr. Featherstone! I cannot, I cannot bear this! I have now lost everything. I am without a mother, without a home, and I have lost my husband, and I have lost my brother. There is one thing to which I clung—your respect; but that also is gone, and yet indeed I do not deserve it.'

'Madam,' answered Paul, 'it is possible that the explanation which would clear your conduct, which is denied to-day, may be afforded in the future. If you can assure me of that, the pity you now command will not be unaccompanied with respect.'

Loveday shook her head sadly. She could give him no hope of such an explanation, at least from her lips. If it came, which she doubted, it would be from Constantine.

'I wish you farewell,' said Paul, sorrowfully, after waiting for a reply. 'We shall probably never meet again.'

He bowed solemnly, and went away. She looked after him with eyes filled with tears. She saw him, when he reached the cottage, unbind *her* kerchief from his head and give it to Tamsin, with a sign that it was to be returned to the owner. But Paul did not look back. Then he took a clean kerchief the daughter of old Carwithen gave him, and that he bound around his head. He would not take away with him any remembrance of Loveday.

She understood his meaning in the action, and it overcame her. She had indeed lost everything—except his pity.

CHAPTER L.

AN APPARITION.

SQUIRE GAVEROCK, Gerans, and Rose were in the room called the study, in which, however, no study was ever undertaken. They were all dressed in deep mourning. Mrs. Gaverock was dead, and had that day been buried. A stroke had fallen on her shortly after the departure of Loveday, which had greatly affected her, and this was followed by another, from which she did not rally. Her departure had been without pain. She had faded away in sleep. How far the Squire had felt his wife's loss none could say. He was not accustomed to show his emotion; it is possible that he did not feel much. ' It is, taken all in all,' said he, ' a happy release. She wasn't good for much of late, and no comfort to herself, let alone others. As for the maidens, she'd lost every mite of control over them. I do not know how it is with others ; but, for my part, I'd be shot or drowned rather than die soaking in bed, dying by inches. But,' he added, philosophically, ' tastes differ, and there is no accounting for them.'

On this occasion he had a bundle of banknotes before him, and a paper.

' Here,' said the Squire, ' you see what your mother's will was, Gerans. She had her money tied up to her ; not much, but something, from eighty to a hundred a year, in the Three per Cents., and one or two other little matters. You see she had left everything to Constantine ; but as he is dead she revoked, and by a codicil left all for life to Loveday ; and I was to dispose of some shares she had in the Bridgewater Canal at once, and pay over the proceeds to Loveday for her immediate necessities. Here is the money, but where is Loveday? She executed a deed of attorney just before the second fit she had to enable the sale at once, and so it was effected before she died, but I have only got the money to-day. Now it is at Loveday's disposal, if I could find her. All the rest of your mother's money—that is, the

money in Consols—will come to you after
Loveday's death. It won't go out of the family.
I have nothing against what your mother did.
Constantine made an ass of himself, and you
must suffer. Eighty pounds a year would have
been something to you ; but, after all, you are
well off, more comfortable than ever I was
with your mother. She, when squeezed as
tight as you could, was not worth quite a hundred, and Rose is worth four without squeezing.'

'Dennis—I mean Mr. Penhalligan,' said
Rose, 'has gone to Exeter to make inquiries.
Loveday has not written, and nothing has been
heard concerning her. When he reached
Launceston, he could learn no news ; she had
spent the night at the King's Arms and gone
on by coach next day, but by which coach and
whither no one had noticed.'

'How did you hear that?' asked Gerans.

'Mr. Penhalligan wrote to me,' she replied,
colouring. 'He knew I was very anxious, and
promised to send me news on the first opportunity.'

Gerans nodded. He was not surprised nor
suspicious. Nothing more natural than that
Rose should desire tidings of her friend and

sister-in-law, nothing more proper than that Dennis should report progress.

'My old friend, Ennoder Hocking,' said the Squire, ' when he was dying was asked whether he would prefer to be buried in the old churchyard or in the new cemetery, and he replied that he would certainly prefer the new ground, because it lay on gravel and was healthier, whereas the old graveyard was on clay and a " rheumaticky place." As for myself, I don't care a farthing where I am buried, but I do care how I die. Bless my soul! what inconvenience and expense there is in a death-bed, and how quick and economical is an accident; no long drawn-out sickness for me, if I may have my choice. But this is neither here nor there, only this I will say, Constantine showed his good sense and good taste in going out of this world in the way he did. No nursing, no doctor's bill, no funeral expenses. I hope it will be the same with myself.'

Rose uttered a cry of terror. She was seated facing the window, and she saw a pale face looking in. The others, startled, turned in the same direction, but observed nothing; they asked her what was the occasion of her alarm.

'I thought—I thought!' she said, in trepidation, 'that I saw Gerans out there, looking deathly white. He looked in through the window glass and fixed his eyes on me.'

'That,' said Gerans, 'is impossible, for here I am in the flesh and in the solid, not very pallid, but fresh in colour.'

Even as he spoke the door behind him opened, and framed in the entrance stood Constantine, so like Gerans, but paler, that all who saw him were silent, startled, not knowing what to think—whether they had before them the ghost of Constantine or the 'double' of Gerans.

'Well!' exclaimed Constantine, 'what are you all staring at me for in that mazed manner? Do you take me for a spectre? Not impossible, you have been eager enough to reckon me among the dead; not an effort did you make to discover whether I were alive. Don't you know me again, father? or has disappointment taken the breath out of your lungs? Gerans, here I am to trouble you again.'

'Good Heavens!' exclaimed Gerans, springing up, and rushing to his brother with open arms. 'Constantine, old fellow! Is this really you? Oh, my God, how glad I am!' He clasped his hand and shook it, then caught his brother in his arms, and hugged him. 'I am rejoiced! Who ever would have expected this!'

'What, Constantine thrown up by the sea!' exclaimed the Squire. 'Humph! come forward, and let me have a look at you.'

Rose gazed on the restored brother with amazement. He was extraordinarily like her husband. Of late Gerans had lost much of his cheerfulness, and this brought him into closer resemblance to the pale, depressed man who stood before them.

'So you are Constantine!' said old Gaverock, without manifesting any exuberant delight at the recognition. 'Always too late for everything. Look here!' He spread out the bank-notes on the table. 'Here are four hundred pounds, the proceeds of the sale of the Bridge-water Canal shares; but they are not for you. There are two thousand six hundred in the Three per Cents., but they are not for you. Just returned too late for the plunder!'

'What do you mean, father?' asked Constantine, whilst his eyes rested eagerly, greedily on the money.

'I mean this, that your mother is no more. And as you chose to keep away and sham dead, she has left her money to Loveday instead. And now we do not know what has become of her. You do not, I suppose?'

'I—how should I know?'

His father looked at him from head to foot. He had been in his boat for some time rowing, had not been able to get much to eat, had been wet and exhausted, and had no appearance of prosperity about him.

'Do you see this?' asked old Gaverock. 'Four hundred pounds in notes, and some small gold and silver over. You don't look to me as if you had had the handling of this sort of thing where you have been.'

'No,' laughed Constantine, contemptuously. 'Where I have been I have not fingered much money.'

'I can believe that,' said Gaverock; and he put the notes away in a pocket-book, and the coin in a purse, thrust them into his library table drawer, locked it, and put the key in his pocket. 'But this might have been yours, had

you not been hiding and made us believe you
were dead. Now, your best way is to find
your wife, and ask her to provide you with a
shilling or two for clean linen.'

'Con,' said Gerans, 'look at Rose. She is
my wife now, and your sister-in-law.'

Constantine held out his hand, but Rose
accepted it without alacrity. His close resemblance to her husband was strange to her.

'You have come from a distance,' she said.
'You are hungry and tired. I will hasten supper.'

'Ah!' said he, 'do so. I have not eaten
anything since early morning.'

'Sit down,' said Hender Gaverock, pointing to a chair on the other side of the table.
'Whence come you? From the bottom of the
sea? The last I saw of you was on the keel
of the "Mermaid," when a sea went over her.
What have you been doing with yourself all
this time?'

Constantine shrugged his shoulders. 'One
thing to-day, something else to-morrow—whatever offered.'

'Why did you not go back to Nankivel?
Why did you not communicate with us? Why
did you let us suppose you dead?'

' Nankivel ! I had had enough of a lawyer's office. I did not write, because I had no pleasant news to tell.'

' That you have not done well is no wonder to me. You are not the man to make a fortune.'

' I'm not an eldest son, born with a gold spoon in his mouth, who gets the property and the heiress.'

His father brought his fist down on the table.

' Whose fault is it that you did not get the heiress, Con ? Your own—you married a beggar.'

' Father,' interposed Gerans, ' what is the advantage of going back to the past? Con is here, alive—that suffices. He is welcome, and we are rejoiced to see him ; if he is unlucky, home is the place for him, where his best friends will endeavour to comfort him. If he had been fortunate, we should have rejoiced. Whether he returns to us prosperous or unfortunate is of little moment, so long as we have him again, risen from the dead.'

' I want to know,' said the old man, rapping on the table again, ' I want to know what he

has been about all this while? It is getting on
for two years since he disappeared. What has
he been about? Where has he been hiding?.'

'I tell you,' answered Constantine, sullenly,
'I have been in various places, trying my hand
at various things. If I was picked up by an
outward-bound vessel for the West Indies, and
went there, and have now come back—what
have you to say to that?'

'Your complexion is not tanned enough for
the sun of the West Indies,' said old Gaverock.

'That shows you know nothing about the
matter. Do you suppose that one can return
in six days from the New World, and bring
one's tanned skin back? The voyage is long
enough to bleach the face; besides, I have
been ill.'

'One can see that,' said Gerans. 'Do not
be unkind to him, father. Poor Con has been
ill, and has suffered. Why, the father in the
parable ran to meet his son when he returned,
and he was a prodigal. Con has not been that,
and you are scarcely gracious to him.'

'Do not you meddle,' said old Gaverock,
angrily. 'I know what I am about. It is not
for the yellow beaks to instruct the parent

birds. I must know all about you, Constantine, before I receive you cordially. The prodigal returned with a confession, and therefore was taken to his father's heart. You come back with evasion and equivocation; therefore I hold you at a distance, with the table between us.'

He continued rapping angrily on the board. His temper was rising. Then he stood up and paced the room with his usual huge strides, with his hands in his pockets. Constantine's eyes followed him. Dusk had set in, and it was becoming dark in the room.

'First of all, you married without my leave, and left me in ignorance of the circumstances. Then you were washed off the keel of the "Mermaid," when I, the older by more than double your years, held on. Then you let us suppose you were dead; and so your mother has willed away her money to Loveday, for her own irresponsible, private, and independent use. Then you come home, without a profession, without money, and, of course, want to be helped on to your feet.'

Constantine looked askance at his father.

'Yes,' he said, 'I do want help. I have

made up my mind to settle in the West Indies. I will have a sugar plantation there, and negroes to work for me; but land and slaves are not to be had for nothing. I have come home to ask you to assist me, and then I will trouble you no more.'

'Loveday is your wife. She has four hundred pounds. You must settle matters with her. I suppose you intend to take her with you?'

'You tell me that Loveday is lost.'

'Yes, but she will be found. Her brother is gone in search of her. People do not get lost for long in England.'

'I do not intend to take her out with me at first, till I have my estate and house; after that, I will write, or return for her.'

'Well, you must settle matters with her. I can give you nothing.'

'I cannot wait till she is found. I have to be off in a few days. I do not wish to meet Dennis Penhalligan.'

'Why not? Are you a coward?'

'I do not wish to quarrel with him. We nigh came to blows before, and we are sure to come to an angry encounter now if we meet.

He is my brother-in-law, and I do not want to
hurt him. In a little while all will be right.
I shall have my sugar plantation and my
negroes, and be a thriving man, with a good
house, and Loveday will be with me; and
then Dennis may come out and doctor my
blacks, if he cannot succeed with white people
here. He is inclined to be my enemy now
because I am down. But when I am up, he
will be amiable enough. No, I will not meet
him. Why should you not give me the money,
father? Loveday is sure to approve.'

'But supposing she does not, then I shall
have to make it up to her. No, no.'

'Then let me have five hundred pounds to
start with. I am your son; you are bound
to provide for me.'

'Did I not pay a premium to Nankivel for
you? Who forfeited that? I have no money
to advance. I am always out of pocket. I
can't sell without Gerans's consent, and if he
consented I would not do it—not reduce the
property for you.'

'Why not? I am your son. Why is
Gerans to have everything and I nothing?'

'It is your own fault if you have nothing.

You were put in a lawyer's office, and on the road to a livelihood, and that opportunity you threw away. I had an heiress for you worth five hundred per annum, and you married Loveday on the sly, and threw that chance away. You were your mother's favourite son and heir to all her money, and you let her suppose you were dead, and so you have lost her money, which has gone to Loveday. Now you are dependent on your wife. Find her, and get her to advance you the five hundred pounds. I will tell you what I think, Constantine. Some men are like skittles, set up to be bowled over. You may set them up a hundred times, and they go over on their sides a hundred and one times. You are one of these. You have no independence of character, no manliness of heart.'

'That is the fatherly reception I get,' sneered Constantine. 'Because I return with empty pockets I am unwelcome; had I come back with a full purse I should have been made much of. I am not the prodigal son of the Gospel who returns snuffling and beseeching forgiveness. I came back to demand my rights, and, by Heavens! I will have them;

and, what is more, you'll be eager to give me
the money to get me off.'

Old Gaverock went hastily out of the room ;
he was so angry that he feared an explosion,
and he had sufficient sense to avoid that on
the night of his lost son's return.

'You must not speak to father in that
manner, Con,' cautioned Gerans. 'He is un-
accustomed to it, and cannot bear it.'

'Pshaw!' exclaimed Constantine, 'he will
have to open his eyes wide before long to
what I say, unless'—he went to the locked
drawer where the money was—'unless he fur-
nishes me with this.'

CHAPTER LI.

WANTED: MONEY!

'WELL,' said Squire Gaverock after breakfast to Constantine, 'what is to become of you?'

Constantine was now dressed in a suit of his elder brother's clothes, and he looked much better than yesterday; he had recovered his colour, and seemed to have filled out. A good sleep after a hearty supper had wrought a great improvement in his appearance. When Rose looked at him, in clothes that her husband usually wore, the resemblance between them was remarkable. The brothers were alike in everything except in the expression of their faces.

'What is to become of me?' asked Constantine. 'That remains for you to decide.'

Gerans was very pleased to have his brother home. He considered him as his natural friend, to whom he could open his heart, and confide the trouble that corroded his soul. He showed Constantine the kindliest, most affectionate sympathy, which the latter accepted without thanks, as his right. Gerans lived in clover, whereas he had to shift for himself on the bare world beyond the hedge.

'I will tell you what will become of you,' said old Hender Gaverock ; 'you shall remain here till Loveday is heard of, and then you shall settle matters with her. If she chooses to let you have the four hundred, she may, and I will add another hundred, which is the utmost I can do. That will make five hundred pounds. With five hundred pounds you shall go to Barbadoes, or wherever you like ; I shall have done with you. You will take your wife with you, or leave her for a year till you are settled. That is the plan. It will do. You shall follow it.'

'I cannot wait till Loveday is found,' answered Constantine.

'Why not? What reasons?'

'I have my reasons.' He looked round. Rose had left the room, only Gerans and his father were there. 'You have your plans, father, and I have mine. I tell you I am off to-morrow, or the day after at latest. I cannot, and I will not, wait.'

' Why not ? '

' I have told you. I have my reasons. That must suffice.'

' But it does not suffice.'

' You had better not ask further.'

' But I do ask further.'

' Then you ask in vain.'

' Then you are a worthless vagabond,' said old Gaverock, in a rage.

' If I am a vagabond, who has made me so? Who but yourself? All your solicitude has been for Gerans; I have been uncon- sidered.'

' That is false. You were sent with Nan- kivel.'

' Yes—when I had not the smallest inclina- tion for a solicitor's office. Of course I am a vagabond. I have no home. I must go over the world looking for one. I have not a house and acres provided for me by my ancestors. They are for Gerans.'

' If you had had a spark of honour in your whole carcass you would not have returned home as you have, after allowing us for two years to believe you dead.'

' If you had had a spark of fatherly feeling in you, you would never have penned me into Naukivel's musty office, with a brick wall to look at, and old parchments to munch. An unnatural father has made a vagabond son.'

Hender Gaverock's face became red as blood, and his eyes sparkled. He grasped Constantine by the collar, dragged him up from his chair, and thrust him down on it again with such violence that the chair gave way, and Constantine fell to the ground.

' I will teach you how a son is to address his father,' said he, and shook his fist at Constantine, who scrambled to his feet with face livid with rage and mortification.

' I have been treated with only violence and insult by you,' said Constantine. ' I ask you for money now, that I may depart out of your sight, never to appear before you again, and have it I will.'

' You will !—how ? '

' Father,' interposed Gerans, ' what can be the harm of granting him what he desires ? He has his reasons, which are no doubt good, that make it necessary for him to leave immediately, and he wants the money at once. A penny now is worth twopence ten minutes hence. Con has told you that he cannot wait.'

'He has had his deserts.'

'No, he has not,' answered Gerans, boldly ; 'you are doing him an injustice.'

'I—an injustice!' The old man flamed up, and Constantine laughed.

'I ask for five hundred pounds. The sum is moderate. I forewarn you, if you do not give me the money willingly, I will make you give it,' said Constantine.

'You! You make me!'

'Yes, I will. If I were to ask for a thousand you would give it with gladness to be rid of me.'

'I should like to see the force you will wield against me, to make me pay money which I do not choose to expend.'

'Do you remember, when I last came here, you tripped me up, father?'

Old Gaverock nodded.

'It is my turn now, and such a fall I will give you as you never experienced before.'

'Con,' interposed Gerans, 'why do you

aggravate father? You can gain nothing by doing so, and your manner is offensive, as your conduct is improper.'

'Leave me to settle my affairs,' answered Constantine, impatiently. 'My father will not give me the money. Is it so?'

'Yes, it is so,' answered Gaverock.

'I will make him do it, with the threat of dishonour on himself, the family, and the name of Gaverock.'

'What! what!'

'Ah! that is my weapon. I must tell you the truth. I have got into a scrape. It was no fault of mine, but let that pass. I am now in danger of arrest and of conviction as a felon, and of transportation.'

The old man uttered a hoarse cry. Like a madman he rushed upon Constantine, who turned pale and started back, and armed himself with a leg of the broken chair. Gerans threw himself between them, laid hold of the furious old man, grappled with and restrained and overpowered him, and thrust him back.

'Gerans!' gasped the old Squire, 'Gerans!' He ceased to resist, and his son let go his hold. The old man panted for breath. Gerans also breathed hard and fast. He was astonished at himself for daring to oppose and control his father, and he cast down his eyes before him, as one that was guilty. He turned aside to his brother, and said, reproachfully, ' Con, you should not say false and idle words certain to anger our father. You know how sacred he holds the honour and name of the family.'

' I spoke nothing but the ugly truth,' said Constantine.

' That,' answered Gerans, ' I will never believe. You are the cleverest and best of us two. I might bungle into wrongdoing, but not you. You have twice as much brains as I.'

' The world is for the brainless, then,' mocked Constantine. ' Towan estate, and an heiress with four hundred a year. I—the clever one of the family—am a vagabond who sues in vain for a few hundred.'

The old man stood looking from one son to the other without speaking, hardly knowing with which to be most angry.

' Father,' said Gerans, approaching old Hender ; but the Squire would accept no sub-mission—he thrust him away with violence, and a smothered oath.

Gerans gave his brother a sign to leave the house, and Constantine threw aside the leg of the chair which he had taken up as a weapon wherewith to defend himself, and went out at the porch door. In another moment Gerans followed him. They walked on together in silence for some distance over the downs towards the sea.

Presently Constantine asked, 'Have you seen mother's will?'

'Yes—that is, I have heard it read.'

'I must have a look at it. I believe it may be upset. She left the money to Loveday conditionally on my death.'

'You need not trouble yourself about that. Loveday gets the money, and she is your wife. It is all the same.'

'It is not all the same. I want the money at once. I cannot wait for it till she is found and can give her consent. I am not sure that she will consent without conditions. How much have you got with Rose?'

'I do not know. I have not looked into matters.'

'I suppose that now her affairs are out of father's hands and in yours. He was her trustee only whilst she was under age and unmarried.'

'I do not know.'

'You can raise money, I presume, independently of his consent?'

'I do not know.'

Constantine laughed contemptuously. 'You do not deserve to have money, if you do not know on what tenure you have it, what is its amount, whether you can dispose of it, whether you can control it.'

'I have had no occasion,' answered Gerans. 'Father is an excellent manager. An agent at Truro manages for Rose; and when that property is sold, we shall buy Dinabole and other land round here so as to have all the estates together within a ring fence. That is father's plan, and I approve of it. Rose does not want to have the house at Kenwyn sold, in which she was born and lived, and if my father insists on that I shall oppose him, but that is the sole point on which any difference is likely to arise. He aims only at doing the best for Rose and me. She knows that as surely as myself, and we are content to trust him.'

'I would trust no one but myself,' said

Constantine. ' However, I am not here to talk
over your plans of rising to be a big county
squire and possibly a high sheriff; your affairs
concern me now only as they touch me. My
necessities are urgent. What I said is true. I
will give no particulars. I am under a cloud,
and must leave the country. I have been
drawn into a horrible quagmire, from which I
must scramble before I am sucked down into
the depth. The money I must have, or in
very spite, to revenge myself on father, I will
let the worst come, and then he will go mad
with shame and rage and vexation that he did
not come to my terms in time.'

' Constantine ! I cannot, I will not, believe
that you have done anything dishonourable.'

' No—the wrongdoing has been forced on
me. You say I have brains. I am easy-going
and good-natured. Easy-going and good-
natured folk get imposed on. I was imposed
on by a hypocritical, pious idiot—and he has
led me into such a trouble that unless I escape
out of the country at once, of my own accord,
I shall be transported out of it, at the cost of
the country.'

' Oh, Con ! '

'What help to me is there in your re-proachful Constantines! and Oh, Cons! I want—not exclamations of righteous or simulated horror, but ready money. In my opinion it is they who lay pitfalls for the unwary who should be punished, not those who fall into them. It is all very well for you to stick to the high road of virtue, because you have no temptations to leave it; you are an eldest son and married to an heiress, but I am nothing and have nothing. I have to get what I can, make a nest like a puffin in a disused rabbit burrow, or catch a meal like a skua from the gulls when they return from fishing by striking them in the breast, making them disgorge, and catching and rushing off with their prey.'

'Brother, this is very dreadful!'

'Of course it is. So is a torn coat, but a tailor will not mend it by holding up his hands over the rent. He must take needle and thread and draw the riven edges together. I want money.'

'What have you done, Con?' asked Gerans, with sinking heart.

'Never mind what I have done. The thing that we have to consider is, what is to be done with me. What do you consider is the thing to be done with a cankered apple-tree in your garden? You get rid of it as quickly as you can, lest the canker spread. I am the cankered tree. You must get rid of me. Mind you, Gerans, it is the soil that produces the canker; the tree is good enough, and the best sorts of apples take the canker readiest. Your sour cyder fruit never catch it. I have not been given proper nourishing soil in which my roots may spread, so I have got the canker. You must 'get rid of me, send me to the West Indies. There I shall recover and bear bigger and better apples than even you with your Towan and your heiress.'

'Have you been, really, in the West Indies, Con?'

'Never mind where I have been. Again your questions are irrelevant. I can assure you I have been in a new world to this, with quite a different order of ideas, and habits, and manners from those of the old world ruled by the Squire of Towan. Where I am going, not where I have been, is that to occupy us at present, and that I do not mind telling you. I am going out of the kingdom, to the West

Indies, and I am going as quickly as I can to prevent being sent east to Botany Bay.'

'I cannot believe this.'

'What? That I am in danger? You will have to arrive at conviction pretty sharply, or the danger will be at your door in the shape of a couple of sheriff's officers to arrest me. I will not wait here much longer. I have some patience with your sluggish minds, which require time to take in new notions, but I will not protract the time indefinitely. Money I want, and will have. Five hundred pounds. If you will give me some of your own—that is, Rose's—or if father will give me Loveday's, it is one to me. The money I must have, and do not so much care out of whose pocket it proceeds so long as it finds its way into mine. If you advance me the money, I will repay it at five per cent. interest out of my sugar canes. If I have Loveday's, she of course will join me, and suck the sugar on the spot out of the canes grown on her gold.'

'You must give me time to think this over,' said Gerans. 'If you must have money, you shall have it. Whatever is mine, personally, I will freely share with you, but I cannot take

Rose's money without her consent, nor can my
father give you the four hundred pounds left to
Loveday without her consent. But, Con ! that
you have been unfortunate I know ; that you
have been guilty, I cannot and will not believe.'

'You have said that already, and I am glad
of your good opinion. As you say, I am unfortunate ; but the self-righteous world will say I
was something else. Well ! when I am on my
sugar plantation whacking my negroes, I shall
whistle across the ocean in the face of this
rotten, canting, hypocritical old world. When
I am wealthy I will come back, and it will
bow low before me and do worship. You will
see ! You will see ! ' He laughed carelessly.
' Gerans, I must have some of the mignonette
seed from under the drawing-room window.
I am passionately fond of the scent of mignonette, and the hot sun of the West Indies will
draw it out in double fragrance. Do you remember the butter-scotch we were wont to
make together, Gerans ? and how little sugar
mother would spare ? You will come out and
pay me a visit on our plantation, and we will
make butter-scotch out of my own sugar,
grown on the estate.' Then Constantine threw

himself down on the short grass. 'I am going no further with you, Gerans,' he said. 'I have a fit of laziness on me, and I will lie and dream here of my sugar plantation. You go on and find out how the money is to be raised for purchasing it.'

CHAPTER LII.

ON THE TURF.

CONSTANTINE lay on the turf, picking up little
empty white shell cases which strewed it, and
crushing them between his fingers. There
was not much sport in this proceeding, but it
was a distraction. Towan was on his left;
from where he lay he overlooked the house.
When he was tired of cracking shells he raised
his head on his right hand, put a stalk of thrift
in his mouth, and tried to tie a knot in it with
his tongue. His eyes rested on Towan, without any emotion at seeing the home of his
childhood again, at the prospect of seeing it
now for the last time.

'If I get to the West Indies I shall not be
such a fool as to return home to my father's
growls, and my brother's exclamations of Oh,
Con!'

His heart was bitter within him at the thought that his brother was well provided for, happily married, exposed to none of the roughs of life, whilst he had to shift for his living, run into, and succumb to temptations. He stood now in peril of transportation, simply because he was a younger son. Gerans was respected as an honourable, just, and generous man, solely because he was the first-born, and as firstborn had everything showered on him for which another must fight. He was angry with Gerans, because he envied his luck. He was angry with his father, because his father was partial. He was angry even with his dead mother, because she had put him to inconvenience by her will, making him subservient to his wife, to whom he did not want to owe an obligation just then. The reception he had met with from his father had not been cordial. He did not stop to inquire whether he deserved a better reception, after showing so little regard for the feelings of his parents as to leave them for nearly two years in ignorance that he was alive. He had returned home, not that home now exercised any attractive spell on his heart, not to see again his old

father and mother, and the brother who loved
him with such sincerity, but because he wanted
money, and knew not whither he should turn
for it beside home. Nevertheless a soft
emotion had risen in his heart on the yester
eve when he came up from the strand, and
saw before him the old walls and roofs, and
his hand had trembled on the door latch before
he pressed it, out of real feeling. But that
was transient, and had given way to bitterness and discontent. He was ashamed of the
momentary melting, as of a weakness. Even
his brother's hearty welcome could not rethaw
his frozen heart. He thought of him only as
one who stood between him and an easy life.

'There is no saying,' said Constantine, spit-
ting the stalk of thrift from his mouth ; 'Gerans
may be dissembling, and be only eager how to
be rid of me cheaply. It is as well that I have
no great tenderness towards him. We shall be
better able to deal with one another in business-
like fashion.'

Lying on the turf and looking towards
Towan, he saw the old Squire ride away on
his favourite cob. Constantine knew it well.
' Whither is he going ? ' he asked, and then re-

membered the day was that of market at Padstow, and the Squire never missed attending.

'It is nothing to him that I am here,' sneered Constantine. 'He is off to learn the price of bullocks and sheep.'

He was wrong in his conjecture. Squire Gaverock was not on his way to Padstow without thought of his son. He was on his way thither to see about raising a hundred pounds for Constantine. He had made up his mind to give him that; more he could not, without selling land, and the idea of selling did not enter his head. 'With a hundred pounds from me, and Loveday's four hundred, and her eighty pounds per annum from the Three per Cents.—it is enough. He must be satisfied. If he has to ask his wife for the money, so much the better; it will make him behave to her with kindness and respect.' Jog, jog, jog! 'After all,' mused the Squire, 'I was a bit sharp with the boy, but he made me angry. Why did he not write and let us know he was alive, and not make his mother miserable?' Jog, jog, jog! 'I don't like his looks. There is a skulking, hang-dog expression in his face which it did not wear in old times.'

Constantine's eyes followed his father along
the Padstow road without love. He was thinking of the four hundred pounds in the old
man's table drawer. That money was his own by
rights. His mother had left it to Loveday only
because she believed her son Constantine was
dead. Morally, if not legally, the money was
his. If he could get hold of that money, he
would be able to settle in the West Indies, and
with some assiduity and determination, and by
keeping the negroes up to their work with a
cat-o'-nine-tails, make a large fortune. There
was no doubt about that, as there was also no
doubt that it would be idle for him to go to
Barbadoes or anywhere else without capital. ' I
am going to be a master, not a slave,' said
Constantine.

Presently he saw Rose come out of the
house and enter the walled garden, carrying a
basket. She left the garden door open—it
was too much trouble to shut it. She went
among the raspberry bushes, and began picking
the fruit. Constantine thought, though too far
off to be certain, that she put quite as many
berries into her mouth as into the basket. In
fact she did so. She had gone into the garden

L 2

to pick for a raspberry pudding. Rose had the
keys of the store-room, and ate the currants
and raisins, and figs, and almonds there whenever she went to the room. She helped herself,
not because she was greedy, but because she
liked sweet things, and liked having something
in her mouth to play with, and she never denied
herself any fancy. So—she liked to see and
talk to and coquet with Dennis Penhalligan, and
notwithstanding his impertinence at the well
she met him and conversed with him, and
allowed him to compliment her, and take
her hand. It was a pastime, and no harm was
meant.

Constantine was so intent watching Rose,
and laughing at the motion of her hand to her
lips instead of to the basket, that he did not
observe the approach of a man from Nantsillan
till he was close at hand—and then he started
as he recognised Dennis. The young doctor
did not go to the house, but walked to the
garden door. Perhaps he judged by the door
being left open who was within. Perhaps as
he went by he caught a glimpse of Rose in her
morning gown. Constantine was interested and
alarmed. He wished he were near enough to

overhear their conversation. He considered whether, if he crept down to the garden wall, he could catch any of it, but he abandoned the thought of doing this ; the wall was high, and of brick. From where he was, he could see what passed ; behind the wall, he would be able neither to see nor to hear.

He saw Rose start with surprise, and take a step eagerly forwards to meet Dennis, then she extended her hand to him, and Penhalligan took and held it for some while.

' Humph ! ' said Constantine, ' on uncommonly friendly terms. To be sure he is her brother-in-law twice removed.'

At last Rose drew her hand hastily away, and began to pick raspberries rapidly. They seemed to have much to say to each other. Constantine looked anxiously. He wondered whether Dennis had obtained a clue to where his sister was. He wondered whether Rose was telling Dennis that he, Constantine, was there. Constantine thought that if Penhalligan made a motion of surprise, he would detect it, and that would assure him that the surgeon had been made aware of the reappearance of his brother-in-law, long supposed to be drowned.

But look as closely as he could, Constantine could detect no such movement. They had other matters to talk about, much more interesting than himself, thought Constantine and laughed. 'And Gerans, the soft-headed, there is no thought of him either, I suppose.'

Just then he saw, but only for a moment, an odd figure of a man in a red waistcoat, that peeped from beneath an oilskin coat, standing in the garden doorway, and at the same time a white spotted dog ran up and down between the raspberry bushes.

The moment Penhalligan saw the dog, he ceased speaking to Rose; he seemed to become excited and angry; he ran after the dog, threw stones at it, and—all at once, Constantine could see neither it nor the red-vested man any more. He supposed that the man had gone along under the wall towards the house, and the dog had left the garden and followed him. The spotted dog had, however, effectually interrupted the interview. Dennis Penhalligan said a few more words to Rose, and then hastily left the garden and returned to Nantsillan. Then Constantine observed that Rose stood by the bushes with her forefinger to her lips in a deep study;

she neither ate nor put into the basket any more raspberries.

If he had been near enough to hear the conversation, he would have been greatly relieved of his anxieties. In the first place he would have learned that Dennis had not come upon the traces of his sister, and that he was altogether following a misleading clue. Penhalligan had assumed that Loveday had gone to Exeter, and he had made that the point of departure for his inquiries. It is true that Madam Loveys had mentioned to him the advertisement, but he argued that if his sister had taken the situation she would certainly have written, whereas it was much more probable that she had found her cousin and was with her. Her cousin was in money difficulties and did not want her address to be known, and had persuaded Loveday not to write to her friends. Consequently Dennis was trying to find out his cousin with the anticipation of discovering Loveday with her. He had returned home unsuccessful, to make some arrangements about his business, intending to leave again after a few days. In the second place Constantine would have learned that Rose had not be-trayed the fact of his being alive and at Towan. The spotted dog had disturbed the conversation and interrupted the current of her thoughts when she was on the point of making the communication to Dennis. Constantine thought that there was something suspicious in this meeting of Rose with Dennis. It was by appointment. The door had been left open purposely. That was his conclusion. 'Well,' said he, 'I can make some use of it, I dare say.'

Gerans had laughed at him half an hour ago for picking up a crooked nail on the road, and asked him what use it could be to him. Then he had replied that it would come handy somehow, and some day. Why was it that Constantine was prepared to lay hold of anything, however crooked, and turn it to his own purposes? of anything that chance cast in his way, and convert it into a weapon wherewith to wound his fellow-men?

'Because,' he would answer, 'I am a younger son.'

Constantine had good abilities, better than Gerans; he had the same lazy good-nature as his brother, a love of taking things easily, but circumstances were against him, and for Gerans.

He had not a fortune to fall back upon. He could not take life easily, he must work to get a living, and he was angry because of this obligation. Why should he, and not Gerans, have to work ?

The day was warm, the sun had heated the sandy soil of the turf on which he lay. He had nothing to do but grumble over the injustice with which he had been treated and find palliations for his own ill-doing. He was tired of lying with his head propped on one elbow, so he threw himself back, put his hands under his head, drew his hat over his face, and went to sleep.

When Gerans came back, he found his brother where he had left him, sleeping and snoring.

Gerans had been thinking since he parted from Constantine. He had not forgotten the reproaches of Rose because he gave way to his father so readily, but he would not oppose the old man without a better reason than to show that he had an independent opinion. Rose was indifferent as to the occasion of a passage of arms, in her eagerness to have a battle in which her husband would measure his strength with his father. Gerans was essentially a peace-loving man, and a just man. He would yield in matters unimportant to insure peace, and he would not oppose his father in matters where his father, he knew, was in the right. He was aware that his yielding to his father had lost him the respect and love of his wife; now the occasion had come in which he would have to take a decided line of opposition. He might not thereby recover his wife's regard, but he would be doing a justice to his brother.

He had a notion that Towan estates were worth in the gross about twelve hundred a year —that is, when all outs were paid, about eight hundred—but he was not sure; his father neither told him the value, nor consulted him about the burdens. There was a mortgage on it he knew for his aunt's jointure, but to what amount he was unaware. There were continual repairs being executed to the farm buildings and cot-tages, but at what annual cost he was not told. The only way by which he had obtained an inkling into the amount of his father's income was through the rate-book which the parish overseer had shown him one day. Whether there were other charges on the estate than the mortgage for Madam Loveys he did not know. What the cost of the maintenance of the Towan establishment was he was unable to conjecture.

His father kept no accounts.

Gerans waited by his brother's side till Constantine awoke. The latter sat up, rubbed his eyes, and asked how long he had been asleep.

'Con,' said Gerans, 'I have thought over what is to be done. When I was married no resettlement of the property was made. Time enough when a boy is born, said father. Consequently, he and I can do with it pretty much what we will. It is of no use asking him to do too much—we must be moderate in our demands —now ; if, after my father's death, I can help you further, and you need assistance, command me. At present I am powerless without his consent. I have resolved to ask him to raise a thousand pounds for you on Towan. Then, with Loveday's four hundred in cash, you will have something to start with, and she will have mother's two thousand six hundred in the Three per Cents.'

'Do you mean this?' asked Constantine, with pleased but incredulous surprise.

'I do, indeed,' answered Gerans. 'You are my brother. Here is my hand, old fellow—is it a compact? I would do more for you if I could.'

Constantine walked on at the side of his brother towards Towan.

'You see, Con, that if I should have no son, the property would come to you. So if you go out of the country, you must not leave us without tidings of you. Towan nearly came to change of heirs the other day when I was samphire-picking for Rose. Penhalligan saved my life.'

Constantine laughed.

There was something unpleasant in the tone of his laugh—a significant innuendo—which jarred with Gerans, and he looked at his brother.

'I have been witness to-day to a meeting,' said Constantine. 'Rose was in the garden picking raspberries when Dennis Penhalligan came to her.'

'Dennis back!' exclaimed Gerans, with glad surprise; 'then he has tidings of Loveday.'

'Possibly,' answered Constantine; 'I was not so unpolite as to run down and form a third in the party.' He spoke mockingly, and Gerans looked at him again, indignantly, whilst the colour rushed to his face. But he was without suspicion of Rose, without jealousy of Dennis; he flushed with indignation at Constantine for reflecting on his wife's proceedings with disparagement. He said nothing more till they reached the house.

CHAPTER LIII.

A THOUSAND POUNDS.

WHEN Gerans and Constantine entered Towan, the former said to Rose, ' What news of Loveday ? I hear from Con that you have seen Dennis.'

' Met him between the raspberry bushes in the garden,' said Constantine.

Rose looked sharply at her brother-in-law ; there was a smirk on his lips and a twinkle in his eye which angered her. She knit her brows, turned her back on him, and answered in a voice tremulous with shame and annoyance, ' No news at all.' Then she went with quick steps towards the door.

' Stay a while,' spoke Constantine ; ' I don't want Penhalligan or, indeed, any one outside Towan to know of my presence here. Will you be good enough to keep my return a secret till my back is turned, which will be as quickly as possible. I shall be obliged if you will silence the servants.'

'I cannot answer for them,' replied Rose. 'Why you should be ashamed to be seen, unless you have done what is discreditable, I do not understand.'

'I explained my reasons to my father and your husband this morning,' said Constantine, coolly; 'as for the servants, their tongues can be tied. Promise them each a crown, if my return be kept secret till this day week.'

Rose made no answer. She went out of the room without another word. She was angry with Constantine and with herself, perhaps a little frightened at the consequences of her inconsiderate conduct. Not a word had passed between her and Dennis to which Gerans might not have listened. Their conversation had been about Loveday, in whose welfare Gerans was as much interested as herself. Dennis had acted, perhaps, injudiciously in coming to her into the garden instead of going to the house, and she had also, perhaps, been unwise in inviting him to come to Towan that evening to see her and Gerans, and tell them his plans for the prosecution

of the search. Penhalligan was reluctant to
enter Towan after his quarrel with the old
Squire. Mr. Gaverock had not quite forgotten
and forgiven the young surgeon for calling him
a bear, though he professed to be content with
the explanation given by Loveday. Dennis
had not apologised, and had not withdrawn
the expression. Therefore he treated him
with coldness, and Dennis would not cross the
threshold unless called in professionally, or
specially invited. He had been summoned to
Mrs. Gaverock when she was taken with
paralysis, but specially invited he had not been
till Rose asked him in the garden. She had
intimated to him that she had something particular to tell him. She had told him nothing
about Mrs. Gaverock's will, nor of the return
of Constantine. Now she thought that if she
had been guilty of an indiscretion, she would
soon put that to rights. She wrote a note :

'Dear Mr. Penhalligan,—Pray do not come
up *this* evening, as I asked you.—Yours very
sincerely,

'ROSE GAVEROCK.'

She sent the note down to Nantsillan by

the postman, who arrived just then, a poor man nearly deaf. Then her mind was relieved. She had done nothing wrong, nothing wherewith to reproach herself.

Constantine and Gerans were in the hall, the latter turning over the letters. The former was at the window.

'Do you employ the postman for carrying messages?' asked he.

'Yes, sometimes,' answered Gerans, with indifference.

'Because I see Rose outside slipping a triangular note into his hand.'

'Very possibly,' Gerans answered shortly; he was hurt and offended at his brother's tone and words.

'Rose,' said he, when his wife came in, 'have you been giving old Hockaday a note?'

'Yes,' she answered.

'To whom?'

'A friend,' she replied, shortly, and left the room.

Constantine laughed.

'She will not be taken to task by you,' he said.

'I did wrong to take her to task,' answered Gerans, sadly, 'I was wanting in good feeling, and she replied to me as I deserved.'

'The wife of Cæsar is above suspicion!' sneered Constantine.

'In every way,' answered Gerans, sharply, 'as gold is untarnishable, because the element of canker is not in it. The cloud covers the mirror from the breath of him who approaches it, the mirror itself is clear.'

Constantine shrugged his shoulders.

'Have you a white liver-spotted dog?' he asked.

'No.'

'Pshaw! because I have seen one about Towan to-day.'

'We have no such dog.'

In the evening Squire Gaverock returned from Padstow. He went into the study where his sons and Rose were seated awaiting him. Since the last sickness and death of Mrs. Gaverock the drawing-room had been deserted by Rose, and she preferred to sit in the library or hall; the former was the snugger room. Old Gaverock was little there. He used the apartment as his office. His box of deeds was there, his desk and money were there, his letters were there, his whips, and guns, and spurs.

He had ridden off his anger, and returned in good-humour.

'Rose,' said he, 'the Kenwyn mine is sold, and the money is in the banker's hands at Padstow. Never had so much gold and notes at my disposal before. I am going to see Tregellas to-morrow about the purchase of Trevithick.'

'I have no objection to the sale of the mine,' answered Rose, 'but I will not have my house at Kenwyn disposed of.'

'I have not said I will sell that,' said the old man, roughly. 'Don't screech before you are pinched.'

'What did you sell the mine for?' asked Constantine.

'For more money than you will ever get, sitting in the corner, twiddling your thumbs. I sold for two thousand five hundred and eighty pounds. Five years ago it would have sold for six thousand.'

Rose was sitting in the window, embroidering the border for the carpet she had promised to Loveday, on which she had been so long engaged.

'Is that money mine now?'

'No, my dear,' answered the Squire; 'I am your trustee and shall invest it for you. You are not to be entrusted with large sums to play ducks and drakes with.'

'Father,' said Gerans, 'I have been considering to-day what is to be done for my brother. You have kept me always in the dark as to the value of this estate, but I can form a rough estimate of what it is worth. There is enough to keep Rose and me here in comfort, and we do not ask for luxuries. The estate has not been re-entailed on my marriage, and therefore you or I can sell or mortgage with mutual consent. It is my wish that Constantine be given a thousand pounds at once, to enable him to buy an estate in the West Indies.'

He spoke quietly and firmly.

Old Gaverock's eyebrows went up to the roots of his hair as he listened to his eldest son.

'A hundred pounds,' he said ; 'here it is. I have raised it this day at Padstow by note of hand. Here it is in gold and paper.' He pulled a purse out of his trousers pocket, and

a book out of the breast pocket of his coat.
Then he unlocked his drawer, and threw in
purse and book. 'There,' he said, 'there is
the hundred pounds I promised. He can have
four hundred from Loveday when he finds her.
He shall have no more.' He slammed the
drawer and locked it.

'A hundred pounds is insufficient,' said
Gerans. 'My mother's money is his and Loveday's, quite independently of what I wish Constantine to have out of the property.'

'You—you wish!' echoed old Gaverock in
too much amazement to boil up with wrath.

Rose put down her needle, and turned her
face towards her husband. She was surprised
at his audacity.

'Yes,' said Gerans, unabashed; 'I have
made up my mind to that sum. You cannot
raise money on the estate without my consent,
and I cannot raise any without yours.'

'I know all that better than you.'

'Well, father, I wish that justice should
be done to Constantine. It is not fair that I
should have everything, and he nothing.'

'He will have his mother's fortune—through
his wife. If he does not have it directly, whose

fault is that but his own, because he allowed her to suppose him dead.'

'That is not sufficient. Besides, he is in immediate need of a large sum of money. He is confident of success in the New World if he lands on it with good capital to dispose of. The least that I can think of letting him have is one thousand pounds.'

'Pray how is that to be raked out of the ground? Are you going to open a cairn, expecting to find a pot of gold?'

'We will mortgage a portion of the estate to raise it.'

'No, thank you. It is well you say we. You luckily cannot do this without my consent, and that shall never be given. I will not allow the property to be further encumbered. I have had trouble enough with the burdens on it. I only shook off some with the aid of money I had with your mother.'

'Very well,' said Gerans. 'If the property was cleared with her money, let the money be repaid to her son Constantine out of it. A thousand pounds, I ask for no more.'

'A hundred!' roared old Gaverock.

'A thousand!' replied Gerans, determinedly.

Rose, sitting at the window, listened with
growing surprise. The man who had yielded
to his father unquestioningly in everything
hitherto, was now showing him a very determined front. What a transformation was
effected in the submissive, pliable Gerans, who
had been ready to slip into a mouse hole before
his father's wrath till now! What occasioned
this change? Surely the love he bore to his
brother steeled him to defy the anger of the old
tyrant. How little love must he have felt for
her, if he had not once stood up in her defence
against the Squire! He was bold in his brother's
behalf, timorous in hers. She was not worth
enough in his eyes to make him measure his
strength with his father, in spite of all she had
said to urge him. His opposition to old Gaverock now, instead of pleasing her, aroused her
resentment. There was another man who loved
her with so fierce a love that he had taken her
part in a trifling matter such as the mounting of
Phœbus, even when he knew she was in the
wrong. How he had held her hand that day,
what fire had flickered in his eyes as he looked
at her, how his voice had quivered with passion
when he addressed her, suppressed, but sup-

pressed with a terrible effort, because he knew
that she would be offended if he gave it vent!
Gerans was not even jealous of Penhalligan's
admiration and devotion. He had accepted
Constantine's hint about the conversation in the
garden, and had received the news that she
sent private notes by the postman, without
surprise and anger. He did not really love her.
He had married her only because he was an
obedient boy, and had been ordered to do so
by his father. She recalled the drive to Wadebridge and the proposal of Gerans, his chin in
a white woollen muffler, and his spotted pocket-
handkerchief to his nose. Then there rose up
before her eyes the scene on the road when
Dennis told her of his love. She uttered a
faint cry. Outside the window was Dennis,
leaning against a side wall, looking at her
through the glass. None of the rest could see
him; she saw his burning eyes fixed on her,
saw the heaving of his breast, saw his hands
convulsively clenched on his bosom, saw how
white and agonised was his face.

None in the room had heard her exclama-
tion. Old Gaverock was storming against
Gerans. He had worked himself up into fury.

Constantine sat in a corner, biting his nails, watching his father ; Gerans, pale but firm, sat opposite the old man, listening to him, waiting till the storm was overpast. None of the three had attention to bestow on her. She made a sign to Dennis, waving her hand, a sign of entreaty that he would go away ; but he would not obey. She looked at him beseechingly, and again waved her hand. What a proof of love was this in poor Penhalligan, that in spite of her commands he would come, if only to get a glimpse of her face through a window ! She was alarmed, however, at his remaining outside. She stuck her needle into the canvas, and began to roll it up ; she intended to leave the room, go outside and entreat Dennis to depart. Just then the door opened, and the servant came in with candles. Rose started up and drew the blinds across the window. She was afraid of the girl seeing outside the face of Dennis. When the lights were brought in the Squire ceased to speak, and waited till the servant left.

Rose's attention had been distracted from the altercation by Dennis's appearance. Now that the curtains were drawn, and he could not see her, he would go away. She leaned her

head on her hand and watched Gerans. His
resolution would fail, she was sure. He made
a little show of resistance, and then would give
way. The storm was broken loose, and he
would strike sail and run before it. But
Gerans did not strike sail as she supposed. He
did not budge from the ground he had taken
up. She listened to him when he spoke, and
was fain to allow that he was right in what he
advanced. He was firm and temperate, but
his cheeks glowed, and his eyes flashed.

'Father,' said he at last, 'the property will
be mine eventually, and I will bear the loss,
not you. I am not only ready but eager to
make the sacrifice, because I consider it
just.'

'You dare to charge me with injustice!'

'I deny that you have treated Con with the
liberality that he has a right to expect of you.
You should not require any urging from me to
do an act of justice.'

'I am not responsible to you,' shouted the
old man. 'Golly! if I had spoken to my
father in the manner you have addressed me,
he would have knocked me down. I will not
give him a penny over a hundred pounds.'

Constantine stood up and left the room. Impotent rage boiled in his heart. He could not remain in his father's presence, and constrain himself. He must go out and cool his heated face, and leave the calmer Gerans to manage for him.

When he was gone, his brother said in a softer tone than heretofore, 'Father, it is not fair that Con should be placed completely dependent on his wife. My mother never intended that. Right is right. My dear mother wished to leave Con her money. You have yourself told me that some of her money was sunk in the property.'

'That was years ago—she has not mentioned that in her will.'

'I know what her wishes were—that all she had, and all she ever had had, should go to Con. I will not accept the freedom bought by her money. Poor Con has had much trouble, has gone through great privations, I fear he has got into some difficulties—I hope he exaggerates their extent. I cannot hold up my head and look an honest man in the eyes, unless I can feel that justice has been done him, and that the wishes of my dear mother have

been carried out.' As he spoke his eyes
moistened, and his tone became soft and pleading.

'I have had a quiet and comfortable home,
and Con has had none at all. I have had plenty,
and he has had poverty. I have my position
secured to me, and he has a position to gain.
I cannot enjoy an easy hour if I know that he
has been thrust forth to hunger and hardship.
It must not be so! Father, your own heart
will tell what I say is right. Give him the
thousand pounds at once. You say you have
got money in the bank.'

'That is not mine—it is Rose's.'

'Very well. Let us mortgage one of the
farms to Rose, and raise on it the sum I want.
Rose!' he said, turning sharply towards her,
'Rose! you will consent to that, will you
not?'

'Yes, Gerans, heartily!'

'There! there!' he exclaimed, almost with
a shout of triumph, 'see what a good, true,
noble wife Rose is. God bless you, Rose, for
that word.'

'Rose has nothing to do with it,' said old

Gaverock. 'Her consent is nothing. I am her trustee, and I will not allow it. What is that?'

Rose was weeping. Why? She did not know, herself.

CHAPTER LIV.

THE SPOTTED DOG.

THE letter received by Dennis from Rose had not had the effect on him she intended. The tone of the note was more than friendly. What did she mean by it? Was it a confession of her own weakness, and dread of seeing him again? Or did she hint that he was not to come openly to the door and ask for admission? He had no rest at home. As the evening closed in, and silvery twilight filled the sky, he was irresistibly drawn to Towan. The moor was silent and solitary. He approached the house stealthily. He looked at the garden door. It was not open, it was not ajar. Then he thought he observed the face of Rose at a window, and he crept nearer, leaned his back against the brick garden wall, where it joined to the wall of the house, and looked at Rose, as she sat engaged on her needlework in the window. The sill of this window was low, a couple of feet above the turf outside. The window had looked originally into the court, but the outer walls of the court, screening the front of Towan manor-house, had been pulled down, so that it was now exposed to the road and moor.

He saw Rose signal to him, and he mis-read her signal. He thought she waved her hand to him to remain where he was, and be quiet, till she came out to speak to him. He waited patiently, without stirring, watching her face till the curtains were drawn. After that he waited on. He could hear voices speaking in the room where Rose was; he could distinguish that of the Squire, it was loud and rough. He thought he could hear as well that of Gerans; but he caught not a word of their conversation. What they spoke about was indifferent to him; he had not come there to hear them argue, but to see and speak to Rose, if only for a minute.

He waited on patiently. Rose would come to him, when she could; she had waved her hand to him through the window in token

of recognition. He was accustomed to wait
motionless by the bedside of a patient, watching a crisis ; so he stood now, not altering his
position. His thoughts were active. How
fate had fought against him ! How cruelly it
had dealt with the lives of two human beings!
It had separated him and Rose, and had bound
her to a man she did not and could not love.
He believed that she hated Gerans, and re-
pented the day that she had married him.
He believed that she loved himself, and himself only. His declaration of love had drawn
from her the cry of 'Too late !' Too late had
she found that she was loved by the only man
whom she loved. He thought of the samphire-
picking. Why had he thrown himself on the
rope and arrested the fall of Gerans ? Why
had he not rather let go and allowed him to
crash down among the knife-like slate rocks?
He wondered at himself. For once luck had
befriended him—had put into his hands the
chance he desired, and he had cast it from
him. Had he not been an inconsiderate, im-
pulsive fool, he would have let the cord whirl
away—and Gerans would by this time have
been buried, and he would not be lingering

there, waiting, hoping, yet knowing that he had nothing to expect but disappointment. All he could look to was to touch Rose's hand, speak a few words about Loveday, wish her a good-night, and go away miserable, despairing, to his lonely home.

He looked at his hands, and then struck them against the wall behind him with such force that they bled. Fool that he was to stand between himself and happiness. Why had he wounded and galled his hands to save his adversary and to perpetuate his wretchedness? His wretchedness! not his own only—that of poor Rose also, chained to an uncongenial, commonplace country clown.

If he had but money, he would carry her off to some distant land, away, by sea, out of the kingdom, and begin with her a new life. But that was not possible. He was poor and powerless. He could hope for nothing more than to see Rose now and then, listen to her sweet voice, and know without expecting to hear her confess that she loved him.

The porch-door opened, and a man came forth. That man was Constantine, but he was dressed in a suit belonging to his brother.

Summer twilight was in the sky, so that Dennis could see though he could not distinguish, and Constantine and Gerans were extraordinarily alike. The young surgeon was startled, and had at once to form a resolution. Where he stood he could be seen. He had presence of mind, and he came forward from his dark corner. Constantine started and drew back; he recognised him at once.

'Gerans,' said Penhalligan, 'I have come up to tell you and Rose that I have ascertained at last the address of my cousin—that is, I know where she is. This day's post has brought me tidings of her. She is at Goodrington, near Paignton. I am off in two days to see if Loveday be with her.'

'Right,' answered Constantine, afraid to speak more than a word or two lest his voice should betray him.

'Rose has told you, I suppose, that my search in Exeter was fruitless?' said Dennis.

'Yes.' Constantine moved to go away.

'I leave on Saturday, and trust at last to discover her.'

'Content.' Then, suddenly, 'Gah!—the spotted dog again!'

In the twilight he saw the white mongrel with its liver patches running round him and Dennis, limping. Then the beast stood up on its hind legs and hopped about them like a kangaroo, then flung itself down on its side as if dead.

'Curse the brute!' exclaimed Dennis. 'That dog will drive me mad. I am haunted with it. Yesterday, in the night, as I drove back from Wadebridge, it sprang over a heap of stones by the roadside at the very spot where I had been upset with Rose on the night of the Goose Fair, and I have not been able to get rid of it since. I see it continually jumping about me, and then disappearing, coming to me when I least expect it; and yet I can never lay hold of it. I have thrown stones at it, but cannot hit it. I have run after it with a stick, but cannot reach it.'

'Shoot it,' said Constantine.

'I will,' answered Dennis. 'See—it is gone!'

The dog had disappeared.

Constantine bowed and withdrew to the house. Dennis was satisfied from his manner that he—Gerans, as he supposed him—was offended.

'It is well,' muttered he—'well that he should understand that I hate him. I cannot dissemble. I am too proud and too thorough to affect love where I hate. Perhaps he knows the reason. It is best so. Best that he should know that he stands between the happiness of two unfortunates whom fate has separated. May be Rose has told him that she scorns and abhors him. It is best so. Best that he should feel some of the misery he has brought upon us.'

He walked leisurely back to Nantsillan. He did not doubt that Rose loved him. Had he not clasped her in his arms and kissed her red lips at the well, and she had forgiven him? Had not her blue eyes told him that she was pleased to see him, and had she not invited him to come to Towan and see her again? Had not her letter shown him mistrust of her own heart? He excused her for not coming to him. She was under restraint. There was a quarrel in the family, and she was the victim. The old Squire and Gerans had been assailing her with reproaches—had been pouring over her vials of wrath and gall. She had borne this for him, because she loved him. She was doomed to a life of daily ill-treatment by two men—the

boisterous, brutal father, the surly, suspicious
husband—because she loved him. For how
many years was this misery to be spun out, her
bright life darkened, her joyous spirit saddened,
her tender heart broken, because she loved
him? Oh, that there were some way of escape
—some means of freeing her from this bondage!

As he came to the dingle down which dived
the path to his cottage, he saw a man standing
at the edge of the wood with a basket slung
over his shoulder by a strap. A crescent moon
was in the sky lying on its back, shedding a
silvery light which, with the summer twilight,
enabled him to see and recognise the pedlar
whom he had first beheld at Wadebridge at
the Goose Fair; but in that uncertain cold
light he could not distinguish the colour of his
waistcoat. The face was very white with the
moon on it, and the Cornish crystal in the band
round his wild, long, black hair flashed suddenly, then was unseen, then flashed again, like
a revolving light at sea.

Something, Dennis could not say what, arrested his steps when he saw this strange man,
and he stood watching him. The pedlar did
not seem to observe him; he was playing or

practising with his long basket. With his hand
he rapped the bottom, and the blow jerked up
the lid, whereupon a number of roses sprang
into the air—white, red, yellow, perhaps, but
in the combined twilight and moonlight they all
gleamed a ghastly white, and fell again into the
basket, when the lid dropped on them and shut
them in. Another rap—up sprang the lid, and
high into the cold light leaped the roses, to
drop again and be shut in by the lid. The
performance was clever. Not a rose fell over
the side upon the ground, nor did the lid close
on the flowers till all were in the basket. The
man was practising, apparently. He tried to
jerk the flowers higher, and each time higher,
and was always equally successful in catching
and securing them. Then he changed his
proceeding. He tapped twice at the bottom,
and now roses and glow-worms shot up out
of the basket, a rain of ghostlike bloom and
pale stars. Tap, tap! and again the mingled
spray was thrown up, again to fall and dis-
appear in the basket.

Dennis stood spellbound; how long he
would have thus remained cannot be said. He
was released from his astonishment by seeing

the spotted cur leap out of the bushes and begin its gambols round the pedlar. Then his anger broke loose.

'You, fellow!' he shouted, 'take that beast away. I have been plagued with it. I do not want either you or your dog in my neighbourhood. Get away with you at once. Leave this place. Take yourself and the brute elsewhere. I warn you—if I see that cursed dog again I will kill it!'

He stepped forward. Immediately, without a word, the man backed before him into the wood, and the dog dived behind some bushes.

'Confound these tramps!' muttered Dennis. 'Why does not Squire Gaverock, who is a justice of peace, clear the neighbourhood of them. Hah! the fellow was not as successful as I thought.'

He saw a pale rose lying on the path in his way, a rose that must have fallen from the pedlar's basket. He stooped to pick it up, but as he stood his shadow was cast over it and the piece of road on which it lay. He groped with his fingers on the ground, but picked up nothing save bits of earth and dust. Then he stood on one side to allow the crescent moon to

illumine the path again. The rose was no
longer there !

He went in at his garden gate, unlocked his
door, and fastened it from the inside. On the
hall table was laid his supper. He lit a candle
and took his place, but he had no appetite, and
he thrust his plate away.

He was by himself in the house. Little
Ruth, after having laid supper for him, was
wont to go away with the woman who came
there to char for him. She slept at her cottage
and returned early in the morning. She carried away the back-door key with her, and let
herself in with it next day. He sat up late,
doing nothing with his hands, but with his head
busy. Of Loveday he thought little. He was
not much concerned about her. He had made
up his mind that she was with her cousin ; she
had discovered her somehow in Exeter, or discovered her address when there, and had gone
to her, and was now at Goodrington. The
journey to Exeter and the stay there had put
him to some expense, and his absence had
interfered with his duties at home. As is usual,
he had been more wanted when away than
when at Nantsillan. Several sick people had

sent for him, and, finding he was absent, had transferred themselves to the old tippling doctor at Padstow.

Dennis considered how different his prospects would have been had Rose been his wife. Comfortably off, unoppressed with the daily pinch of poverty, with her presence as sunlight in his home, all the darkness and burden of his life would have rolled away. Then from out of his burning, dry heart there welled up a fiery spring of hate against Gerans. He, and he only, was it who had spoiled his life, stolen from him the woman he loved, deprived him of the money which would have made him easy in his circumstances. He had nothing to live for now — nothing — nothing — and that was Gerans's doing! He would have liked to have his enemy there, in the dark room with him, and to have fought him. His nerves quivered with pleasure at the thought of striking Gerans, of beating him down, of hearing the thud of his head on the slate floor. He stood up, with feet apart, and imagined himself standing above Gerans, with the life of his enemy in his power. Would he spare him? Dennis laughed aloud. When he laughed, then a dog outside barked, a strange bark like a laugh, or the echo of a laugh. Dennis went to the window and looked out. He could see no dog. He saw the moon twinkling among the swaying boughs and leaves of the oak wood, and the flickering lights on the ground like white dancing roses. Then he went upstairs to bed. But though he lay in bed he could not sleep. He had retired at midnight. The crescent moon was gone, or no longer shone in at the window. The wind sighed outside among the trees.

All at once, he started and raised his head. Against the whitewashed wall at the foot of his bed he thought he saw something move. The moon had not set; it had not shone into his room because of a dense mass of ivy-hung elm and a holly that had obscured it. Now it passed from behind these bushes and flared between some boughs, making a grotesque figure on his wall that waved and moved as the branches and leaves waved and moved. The freakish light drew on his wall a figure like a white dog sitting up on its haunches, with its paws before it, begging, and the head bobbing and turning, the paws now thrust forward, then drawn in as though trying to reach some object, and failing. Moreover, the white dog was covered with moving liver spots. The head was at one moment very distinct, with a brilliant eye, then it was blurred and shapeless, then it was turned aside and clear again. The beast seemed to put up its paws and wash its face as a cat or a rabbit, and the ears flapped as it turned its head. All the while the liver spots ran over the body, melting into each other, dividing, disappearing, then manifesting themselves again.

Suddenly the fantastic figure was gone, the wind rushed past the window, and whilst the wind rushed there was no white dog on the wall, but a whirl of white roses flying up and down fast, faster, up and down and in and out, some falling on the floor, some sprinkling their petals over the bed, but all gathering themselves up again, the petals rejoining the blossoms that shed them, and dancing like a spin of snowflakes.

Dennis threw himself back on his pillow. His mind was overwrought, his nerves unstrung; he was becoming a prey to fancies.

The gust of wind was gone; there were flickers of light and moving spots of shadow on the wall still, but no shape. He watched them till they went out, one after another. Now, certainly, the moon had passed beyond the house, or behind so dense a mass of foliage as not to cast shadows and lights in his room. So he thought, but was presently undeceived by seeing one gleaming spot, one that seemed to shine and twinkle like the Cornish crystal in the pedlar's hair. This spot appeared on the wall and travelled along it slowly. Dennis followed it with his eyes. It was formed, doubtless, like the rest of the fantastic figures, by the moon among the branches and leaves; but it was certainly strange that on this occasion there was but a single light. It crept along the whitewashed wall very stealthily. It seemed to travel like a snail, and at a snail's pace. All at once it flashed with double brilliancy. It had touched and was gleaming on the little double-barrelled pistol Rose had given to Dennis on the night of the Goose Fair!

CHAPTER LV.

AWAY!

NEXT morning, early, Squire Gaverock departed on his cob, along the Padstow road. He did not say whither he was going, or what business took him from home; he was out of humour with both his sons, would speak to neither, and merely told Rose curtly that he would not be home to early dinner, unless he got through what he had to do much quicker than he expected. Gerans also went out, in the direction of Nantsillan, after informing Rose that he intended seeing Dennis—for what purpose he did not say.

Thus Constantine was left alone with Rose in the study.

'Gone down to Nantsillan, is he?' said the former. He was sitting half on the table, but his foot was on the ground—the right foot;

the toe of the left rested on the top leather of
the right boot. He wore a pair of Gerans's
hunting-boots, with red leather tops. He had
on his back a blue coat with brass buttons, his
brother's best coat. Gerans had told him to
make free with his wardrobe, and he had taken
him at his word. He had on, as well, a white
nankeen waistcoat, and a fine shirt with a frill
—all of the best that he could rummage out of
the drawers and cupboard of Gerans. He had
a stick in his hand, and with the ferrule he
played with the toe of his—that is, his brother's
—boot. Only Gerans's best boots fitted him ;
those at all worn would not accommodate
themselves to his feet.

'Gone down to Nantsillan, is he?' asked
Constantine. 'I am not surprised. Gone to
have it out with Dennis, I presume.'

'Have what out?' asked Rose. '*It* is vague,
and refers to anything without life.'

'Plenty of life in this matter—a little exu-
berance mayhap.'

'I do not pretend to understand you,' said
Rose, tossing her head and curling her lip.

'Probably you pretend *not* to understand
me.'

'You take liberties to be impolite, trusting to your kinship, and to my husband's placidity of temper.'

'Oh ! that placidity is ruffled, and may toss and foam. You are indebted to me that I did not work him into breakers this morning, by telling him that your gallant was hanging about the house last night under the windows, waiting for you to come out; but the naughty Gerans was within, and would not let you escape.'

'You are a bad, insolent man,' exclaimed Rose, in shame and disgust.

'The meeting in the garden was not enough by day ; you must meet again by the garden wall at night.'

He laughed, but his laugh was silenced by the flaming indignation in her eyes. She was swinging herself out of the room, when he caught her by the wrist, and said :

'I have not told Gerans, but I will, unless you pay me to be silent.'

Rose did not understand him, though he pointed with his stick to the drawer where his father had locked up the money.

'Say what you like,' she answered, dis-

engaging herself from him. ' Speak the truth
—I am not ashamed of that—but hint nothing
from your evil heart.'

Then she left the study and ran to her bedroom, where she locked herself in to weep her
heart out. Her feelings were in tumult, swaying her from side to side. Everything rocked
about her, and the ground rocked under her
feet. She saw now how foolish, how inconsiderate she had been, to put her character in
the hands of one so unscrupulous as Constantine.
She had trifled with the thoughts of Dennis's
love for no other reason than that his devotion
flattered her vanity.

When she was gone, Constantine took the
handle of the drawer and drew at it. The
drawer was locked and resisted his efforts.
There were five hundred pounds in there.
Gerans offered to get a thousand for him, but
Gerans had shown his powerlessness the evening before. Should he wait another day, and
allow Gerans to plead for him again ? He was
by no means sure that his brother was in
earnest. No man who was not a fool would
burden his estate with a thousand pounds if he
could help it. Of course Gerans affected to

desire it, as a decent show of fraternal love is
expected by the world; but there was no
reality in his effort, no sincerity in his protesta-
tions. No man, said Constantine, can fatten
on promises. A sprat in the net is worth more
than a whale in the sea.

He threw himself into his father's chair, and
stretched out both his legs before him, and
tapped the toes of his boots alternately with
the ferrule of the cane, whilst his eyes rested
on these same toes. His brows were knit, and
his forehead full of creases. He thrust out
his lips. 'For good or ill,' he said, 'I wish I
were in my brother's boots—metaphorically as
well as really.' Constantine's character had
deteriorated rapidly of late. Three years ago
he had been a pleasure-loving, careless, good-
natured young fellow—selfish, disliking the
drudgery of work, but without harm in him.
Then came the initial wrong done in marrying
Loveday clandestinely. From that moment he
had taken a downward turn, and his path had
become precipitous of late. He had allowed
himself to drift into moral ruin; he had not
run into it wilfully. He had never harboured
bad intentions, had always desired to do what

was right, but had lacked the energy to act on
what he knew was right, till the perceptive
moral faculty was dead within him. He was now
incapable of seeing what a base and despicable
ruffian he had become. The old father was
not free from guilt in this disintegration of his
son's character. His despotism exercised over
the lads whilst their characters were forming
had injured both, had deprived both of self-
reliance and spontaneity.

Constantine had in his pocket the crooked
nail he had picked up on the road, when walking outside the house with Gerans. Now he
found a use for it. He put the nail to the
drawer lock, and in another moment the money
that had been left by his mother to Loveday
was before him—that and the hundred pounds
his father had undertaken to give him—five
hundred pounds in all. His hand trembled
as he turned over the bank-notes, his face was
white as chalk, and cold drops beaded his brow
and upper lip. But he was able to pacify his
conscience. He was taking what was his own.
His mother had intended him to have it. She
had left it to Loveday under an erroneous
belief in his death. Besides, it was his anyhow,

for Loveday was his wife, and between husband
and wife there is no mine and thine, or rather,
on the side of the husband, ' thine is mine, and
mine is mine '—all take and no give. He put
the purse with the gold and the two pocket-
books away in his breast, shut the drawer, and
stalked out of the room, whistling. He looked
round in the hall for Rose. If she had been
there he would have told her some lie to excuse
his absence from dinner. His father would
not be home till the afternoon. Gerans was
away. Gerans would not think of examining
the drawer. Rose would be too busy about
household matters. He had several hours
during which he could escape; but, he thought,
it would not do to depart in the boat in Gerans's
best blue coat. He would, indeed, take that
with him; but for the rough work of rowing
he would wear something less fine. So he
went upstairs, took off the coat and waistcoat,
and put on a common every-day suit that also
belonged to Gerans, rolled up the blue coat
and nankeen waistcoat in a bundle, and went
off over the downs towards the cliffs, with his
bundle in hand. The boat in which he had come
from Stanbury—Paul Featherstone's boat—

was not in the boathouse at Sandymouth ; he had come into Nantsillan Cove, and had run his little craft into the Iron Gate, and drawn it up on some sands there, which were not submerged except in a storm. When he had gone a little way along the down, as if on his way to Sandymouth, he struck a different course and came round towards the steep goat-path that led down the face of the crags to the bay into which the Nantsillan brook discharged itself in a pretty fall. He had quite made up his mind what to do. He would row to New Quay, and leave the boat there. Thence he would strike inland by Truro, and cross the isthmus to Falmouth, whence he could easily and quickly get out of the country. Whether there were packets or sailing vessels bound for the West Indies from Falmouth, or that put in at Falmouth, he did not know. That he could ascertain when he got there. More pro-.bably they ran from Bristol. But that was a matter of minor consideration ; his great desire now was to leave the kingdom as expeditiously as possible. Whither he went concerned him less ; with five hundred pounds in his pocket the world was open to him.

'There is Canada,' said he to himself, ' but I don't fancy it. The winters there are very cold, and I dislike cold. There are the States —but I should have to work hard there, and I am not partial to work. Then, turning in another direction, there is New South Wales, but I do not fancy the society there—a bad type of men, the scum of England, convicts, rag-tag—not the sort I could associate with. No, first thoughts are best thoughts, and the cream comes to the top when the milk is sweet. I'll go to the West Indies—perhaps Jamaica, perhaps Saint Domingo, perhaps South Carolina —anywhere where there is negro labour, and there are sugar-canes. I always had a sweet tooth ; I had rather grow sugar than anything else. How Gerans and I loved treacle-pudding as boys ! By George ! I'll go to the West Indies, I will ! ' After a while he began to consider about Loveday. ' She is too finical in her ideas. I am very fond of her, and she will have two thousand six hundred in the Funds. There is this disadvantage, that she knows my unfortunate story, and might throw it in my face at any time. Perhaps it would be advisable to begin the new sum with a fresh slate ;

on an old one, however rubbed, the figures come through and confuse the reckoning. I am very deeply attached to Loveday, and she is my wife. If I am an exile, it will be a pleasure to have some one to speak with who knows about the old place, and with whom one can talk of former times—pleasant times before this wretched muddle came about. Besides, I must have some one to cook and stitch, and knit my stockings. I think I will send for Loveday. Yet, perhaps it will be wisest for me to see how I can get on without her first. If I want her two thousand six hundred I can always fetch her over. If I find I can do without, well, I shall be unencumbered. This is settled ; Loveday waits on my convenience. The woman was made for man, and not man for the woman. She has caused me annoyance and heartache and mental worry enough at Stanbury and Marsland. It is well that she should suffer a bit for it, and learn by punishment not to be self-seeking.' He strode on a little further, and his thoughts took another direction. He laughed. ' Curse it,' said he, ' I am sorry to go without enlightening Gerans's mind about that little pretty coquette, Rose.

He is without a suspicion. I wish I had told
him that I found the doctor lingering under
the garden wall last night. I owe Gerans a
kindness. I will write to him when I reach
Falmouth, and post my letter just before I step
aboard. I will tell him all I have seen, and
what I suspect. Then there will be a storm in
Towan. I should like to be there to witness it.
However, one cannot fire a gun and stand by
the target and see the shot strike.' He was now
very near the head of the path where it descended the precipice. ' I wonder,' he said to
himself, ' I wonder what Gerans had to say to
Penhalligan this morning. He looked grave
when he went off, and intended something more
than to invite him to go out fishing or row after
seals. If he was going to call him to order for
casting sheep's-eyes at Rose, there will be an
ugly end to the meeting, for Dennis is violent
when his blood is up, and Gerans, for all his
quietness, is deuced determined when his honour is touched. I would give a crown to be
present at that interview; but we cannot have
all our wishes gratified, and I have got five
hundred pounds in my pocket, and the sea is
before me.'

Constantine descended the path in the face
of the rock very warily. He was accustomed
to cliffs; he could look down without losing his
head. Some people can climb up more easily
than descend; it was not so with Constantine
in more ways that one.

'I think,' said Constantine, as he crept
down, holding by one hand to every projection
of rock available, and trying the path before
him with his foot before he rested any weight
on it, 'I think it both a queer and an unfair thing
that Gerans and I should be as like as two
acorns growing on one stalk, and yet that he
should have the sunshine and I the shadow, he
the luck and I the loss.'

He reached the shore in safety. 'Ah!' he
growled, 'the tide does not quite suit. There
is a fatality against me. I cannot get the boat
out for another hour—perhaps more. I must
go into Porth-Ierne, and lie hid there, and be
ready to float the boat as soon as the water
rises. No one will dream of looking for me
there; besides, the money will not be missed
till father returns, and that will not be till
afternoon.'

He jumped upon the ledge of slate rock that ran into the tunnel scooped by the waves through the promontory of Carduc, and disappeared within the vault.

CHAPTER LVI.

A SHOT.

Gerans Gaverock walked to Nantsillan. The morning was bright, and every bush in the glen was hung with dewdrops, that twinkled prismatically in the early sun. Near the sea the dew falls of a clear night heavily, and beads the twigs and grass with drops as rain.

Gerans's face, as Constantine had remarked, was serious. He was not going to tell Penhalligan that Constantine was there, because his brother did not wish it, but he was determined to let him know that Loveday was not a widow, as he and she supposed.

'Where is your master?' asked Gerans at the door, of little Ruth, who answered the knock.

'Master hev a-gone out and about wi' a pistol,' answered the girl. 'There hev been a queer white spotted dog about the place yester-

day and all night and this morning, sure
enough, a-worriting of master. He hev a-took
on terrible, and he've gone out to shoot 'n.
Nobody seems to know nothing about the dog;
her don't belong to nobody, seemings.'

'Which way has Mr. Penhalligan gone?'

'Down the coombe, your honour. But, sir,
don't you go for to run in the way when he's
a-firing. It be the spotted dog he's going to
kill, and master 'd be terrible put out if he
shot you instead o' the dog.'

Gerans looked at the little garden before
the cottage as he went through it. The absence
of Loveday's hand was perceptible. The white
jasmine had broken away from its ties against
the wall, and was fallen over on a flower-bed;
the Canterbury bells had been beaten by wind
and rain, and needed binding to a stick. Weeds
had sprung up among the garden flowers, and
daisy-leaves appeared with grass in the paths.
Even the gate, and the doorstep, looked un-
cared for, and the window-glass was not clean
in a climate where encrusting salt from the sea-
air has to be incessantly rubbed away.

Gerans walked slowly down the glen towards the cove, looking on all sides for Pen-

halligan. The little stream, running among ferns and under trees, emerged from shadow, and danced sparkling over stones, where the grove abruptly stopped at a turn of the valley and gave place to short turf and furze. The point where exposure to the prevalent north-west wind began was marked as sharply as with a knife. The trees were arrested, and the sea-grass and thrift began. The air was light, the sea blue, and the hills primrose in the soft sunlight, with here and there a cobalt shadow cast by a white cloud on the down sides, indigo when on the sea. Gerans now saw Penhalligan before him, and he called. Dennis turned. He had the pistol in his hand. He saw that Gerans's eye was on it, and he explained the reason of his carrying it.

'Do you remember that pedlar at the Goose Fair? He had a white spotted dog. Well, that dog has haunted me of late. I see it everywhere. It runs round me when I walk. I hear it outside my house. I dream of it in my bed. It stood this morning on my door-step looking in on me, then it scampered off. I will make an end of the brute. I will be pestered with it no more. It has gone this way, I believe, but I do not see it at the moment.'

'The pistol is loaded?'

'Oh yes, both barrels; if one fails the other shall not.'

'Never mind the dog. Come on with me, Dennis, down into the cove, or to that rock by the fall, where we can sit in the sun together, and talk. I have something I want to say to you very particularly.'

'I am at your service. My time is not in such requisition that I cannot spare an hour. Besides, Ruth knows where I am should any one come to the surgery for me.'

'I have not had an opportunity of speaking alone to you since Loveday left,' said Gerans. 'No news of her, Rose tells me.'

'None.'

'Are you going to seek her again?'

'Yes; to-morrow. I think she is near Paignton with her cousin.'

'You think; you are not sure?'

'I am not sure; I suspect.'

'I shall sit here,' said Gerans, letting himself down on a stone. 'I like to hear the plash of the water. Sit down also, Dennis.'

'Thank you. I prefer to stand.'

Gerans sat musing in the sun ; his pleasant, good-natured face was troubled now ; he wanted to tell Dennis that Constantine was alive without allowing him to suspect that he was then at Towan. He was so open in character and frank of speech that he had great difficulty in keeping anything concealed. He was now considering how he was to tell half the truth.

'You think you will see Loveday shortly?' he asked.

'I consider it probable.'

'Give my love to her. I always have had the greatest regard for Loveday. She is so noble, so good, so true.'

Dennis said nothing in reply.

'Tell her that I hope by the time she returns, or, if she does not return, by the time we know she is settled somewhere, I may be able to give her an agreeable surprise. Probably the very pleasantest surprise that could be given her. Can you guess, Dennis?'

'Not at all.'

'Well, only tell her that, no more. It will set her mind working, and her loving heart fluttering.' He looked up. 'Dennis, turn the mouth of the pistol another way, will you? It is aimed now right at my heart. You are a nervous being, and your finger might twitch the trigger involuntarily if I said something to surprise you very much, and—that would be bad for both of us.'

Penhalligan averted the barrel, and muttered something which Gerans did not catch. But Gerans looked attentively at his face, and said, 'Dennis, old fellow, you are out of humour with me. You have been so for some time; you have avoided me, and have answered me shortly. By the Lord! if we are not friends it is a pity—close neighbours, and meeting each other daily; not so only, but brothers-in-law. Come, Dennis, sit down on that stone, and tell me how I have offended you.'

Penhalligan's face darkened. His brows drew together. Instead of complying with the request of Gerans he planted himself more firmly where he stood, with one foot on the path, the other on a stone, and folded his arms, the pistol thrust forth out of his right, pointing behind him towards the crags of Carduc. He made no other answer to Gerans.

'Well!' said the latter, 'this is not the best of fellowship. However,' he sighed, 'I have no complaint to make against you; it is you who have occasion against us. That is why I am here now, Dennis. That is what I want to speak about. I have been thinking a great deal of late about your sister, and I see that she has been ungenerously, even cruelly, treated by us. I ought to have seen this before. I did see it in a vaporous manner, but now I see it all sharp and clear before me. I have leaned too much hitherto on my father's judgment, and taken his opinion as infallible. I acknowledge my mistake. A man must think for himself, and do what is right according to his own conscience, not according to what another thinks is right. That has been my weakness, but I see it now, and will fight against it. I do not like to resist my father; I do not like to suppose he can be wrong; but still—it is inevitable that we should not see duties alike.'

'To what does this preface lead?'

'To this, Dennis. I have resolved to let all the world know the relationship in which Loveday stands to us. It is all very well for

my father to banish her for a twelvemonth,
and say that he will take a year to decide
whether he will acknowledge her or not. I
acknowledge her as my sister. I have a voice
in the matter as well as he. I have a conscience
which tells me it is a shame and a sin to
conceal this any longer, and to impose hardships on poor Loveday. My God! it is an
honour to us to have her for our relative. If I
have occasion to be proud of anything, it is of
that. She is a noble girl, and I will hold up
my head at the thought that she is my sister.
I think I esteem her even more highly than do
you.'

Dennis shrugged his shoulders, and said
nothing.

'I have had a passage of arms with my
father,' continued Gerans, 'about another matter, in which he was in the wrong and I in the
right, and to my astonishment I have carried
my point. We differed about the raising of a
thousand pounds on the property, and—will
you believe it?—after a hard fight he gave
way, gave way all at once, and has gone over
to-day to Padstow about the money. Now,
I am well satisfied that Loveday has been

unfairly dealt with by us Gaverocks. It all
began with Constantine. I did not like to
speak against him when I thought him dead—
that is, not at first, but I felt that he had acted
very wrongfully by her. Now I do not mind
saying this plainly. It is from us that expia-
tion should come. We have injured Loveday,
not Loveday us. Constantine trapped her into
a clandestine marriage, and held her by a
promise of silence under false assurances; he
assured her that he would tell his father about
their union, and he failed to do so. Loveday
fulfilled her part honourably; Constantine be-
trayed the trust she had placed in him. This
is clear to me now as Cardue Point, and it is a
truth not tunnelled through and liable to be
broken down like Cardue Point.'

Gerans paused, and looked up at Penhalligan. The same gloomy frown was on his
face; his arms were folded tight, his hands
clenched, his lips were drawn over his teeth,
and were white.

'I dare say you have felt that we have
used you badly,' pursued Gerans. 'I consented to hold my tongue because Loveday
urged it. But I ought not to have listened

to her. It was weak in me to give way.
That you have resented our behaviour I am
well aware. I have seen how you have drawn
away from me and have declined my friendship.
That has gone to my heart, and I have felt
it the more because I knew it was deserved.
Now, Dennis, I ask your pardon. I will keep
silence no longer. This very evening I will
have the matter out with my father, and Loveday shall have right done her, full and immediate. I go over to-morrow to Madam
Loveys to tell her everything, and through
her I trumpet the truth to the entire neighbourhood. It will be in vain for my father
to oppose me; I will carry through what I
now know to be right. But that is not all;
there is more to be told, only not yet. You
must have patience, Dennis, and in a week at
furthest you shall hear additional news which
will surprise and please you. Have you been
told that my mother has left all she had to
Loveday?'

'No. I was away when your mother was
buried.'

'She has left her four hundred pounds in

cash, and two thousand six hundred in the Stocks.'

Dennis turned and looked at Gerans with surprise.

'It is true,' said Gerans; 'my father is executor, and has the money ready for Loveday directly she is found. I am delighted at this, and it will help to reconcile my father to the view I take.'

He waited, expecting Penhalligan to say something; as he did not, Gerans went on, with increasing eagerness and some emotion: 'There, Dennis! You know now that I will do all that is honourable and just towards your sister. It has not been done before this because I have been—yes, I will confess it—a coward. I gave way to my father in everything, without weighing my own responsibility. You may believe me, Dennis, when I assure you that I have been brought to see my weakness, and to make this confession, by having suffered in a way you do not know, but which has been very cutting to me. I have had to undergo punishment, and my sentence is not yet worked out; however, I will bear it, and do better. Now give me your hand

Dennis, old fellow, and let us be best friends again.'

He stood up from the rock on which he had been sitting and held out his hand towards the surgeon.

'Take it away,' said Dennis, hoarsely, 'I am not a hypocrite. I will not promise what I cannot give.' He quivered with emotion. He saw that by striking Gerans in the chest he could upset him over the edge of the rock, and that then Gerans would fall down the steep cliff and be broken in every bone.

Gerans looked at him with surprise. 'Dennis,' he said, gravely, 'no one, not even my deadliest enemy, would have offered me his hand and asked pardon, and been refused.'

'How do you know that I am not your deadliest enemy?' cried Dennis, in a sudden outburst of hate and rage.

'My enemy!—and yet you saved my life?' said Gerans, shaking his head.

'Cursed, cursed to all eternity be the moment in which I did that!' exclaimed Dennis, in a paroxysm of jealousy and fury. 'I hate myself for having done it. Go along with you, I tell you, go whilst you may. Beware of me! I am dangerous! There is no more room on earth for you and me.'

His words, his face, the twitching of his hands, one of which held the deadly weapon, showed a conflict of dread and desperation in his heart.

Gerans looked him firmly, questioningly, in the eyes. Dennis turned his face away. He could not meet his look. Then Gerans reseated himself on the stone, and hid his face in his hands.

After a few minutes of mutual silence, Gerans said, in a voice that shook, 'Dennis, you do not bear me this hatred on account of your sister?'

The answer of Penhalligan was a groan.

What was there in the tone of this utterance that made Gerans look at his companion with a face that grew cold and livid with horror? The secret of Dennis's soul was revealed by that moan. The truth, to which he had been so long and so unaccountably blind, was disclosed by it to Gerans. If Dennis loved Rose, then, indeed, all hope of reconciliation was over.

He stood slowly up, and without a word

went up the path towards the coombe. He must be alone with the anguish and terror that tossed and tore in his heart.

His silence and his departure showed Dennis that his love had been discovered. The die was cast. Never again could he and Gerans meet. He could no more go up to Towan and see Rose. If he had thrust Gerans over the precipice, even then, when the truth burst on him, and he was stunned with the discovery, the riddle would have been solved, Rose have been free, and himself on the way to happiness ; but when, for the second time, the life of his rival had been in his power, he had not seized the opportunity. 'Woe be to him if he gives me a third chance !' exclaimed Dennis.

Then he descended the steep path to the bay. He would pace the sand, and consider his course. The image of Rose stood before him, in her pretty white dress with a blue sash, her golden hair, her forget-me-not blue eyes full of sparkle, as she stood before him in the glade carpeted with dead leaves, holding the four-leafed shamrock, and bidding him not despair. He flamed at the vision. His blood went in scalding waves through his arteries.

She was not happy; she could not be happy with Gerans, because she loved him, Dennis. He fancied he heard her voice above the swash of the rising tide, that lapped the sand, and stroked it, and withdrew, to lap again, 'Save me! release me! Dennis!' He fancied her extending her delicate arms towards him, love and longing on her red lips, in her gleaming eyes.

What salvation was possible for Rose? None, save through the death of Gerans, and twice had he put from him the chance of freeing her without grasping it.

The sun was hot; fevered with his thoughts, teased with the roughness of the beach, that was cut through with vertical reefs of slate, he looked for shade, where he could rest and be cool. He stood by the projecting portion of the slate ledge that ran some way into the Porth-Ierne tunnel. He mounted the ledge. In the gloom and chill of the Iron Gate he would sit and think what was to be done. He crept along the shelf, and suddenly—confronted the man he hated.

The gulls in Nantsillan Cove were startled by a report—it sounded like that of a gun—

from the depths of Porth-Ierne, and the echo was caught and beaten back by the cliff opposite. Then Carduc took the echo, and flung it back at Sillan Head. And so the opposite crags played ball with the report, till it grew so faint and small that they threw it away.

The reverberations were not done when a man rushed out of the cave, leaped from the shelf, and crossed the sands hastily towards the path that led to Nantsillan.

CHAPTER LVII.

ANOTHER SHOT.

'HERE I am,' said old Gaverock, bustling into the hall, with his coat tails pinned forward, his riding-whip in hand, his top-boots on his feet. 'Back for dinner after all. I rode right on end into Padstow, went into the bank, settled my business, and here I am again. Rose, all is settled famously. Con shall have a hundred pounds to start with, and as soon as he gets to Barbadoes, or Jericho, or Botany Bay—wherever it is that he intends to set up—then he shall have nine hundred. I've not a word to say against Gerans for sticking up to me as he did last night. If a man has an opinion, let him flourish it, and not throw it away. I respect him for it. Gerans will be a man yet. Where is he, Rose? The bell has rung. I heard it as I came along the down. Heigh! some one, ring the house-bell again. The boys

are out in the stable-yard may be, and so engrossed in the horses that they cannot hear.
In my time I was always hearty for my dinner,
never missed a meal, and was first in my place
at table. Ring the bell! But, Rose, we will
begin. I wait for no man. What is it? Roast
mutton?'

The Squire was in good spirits; he talked
incessantly during dinner, interrupting his conversation at intervals to inquire after Gerans
and Constantine. It appeared to Rose that he
had come round to the opinion of his eldest
son about giving Constantine the large sum
asked for him, but he did not like to admit it;
he pretended that he yielded because the real
person to be pinched would be Gerans, not
himself, and that he could not stand in the way
of a man nipping his finger in a door, if he
chose wilfully to nip it.

Rose did not share the old man's spirits;
she had been so much disturbed by Constantine's insolence in the morning, and by the rude
awakening of her conscience that had resulted
from it, that she was depressed, and, although
she would not admit it to herself, uneasy at the
absence of her husband. Gerans had gone to

speak in private about some serious matter to Dennis. Was she the subject of their talk? Would she be the occasion of a quarrel? Had she by her folly nourished the hopeless passion of Dennis, and alienated from her the heart of Gerans? Her eyes were red with tears, but the Squire did not observe this.

'Run,' said she to one of the servants, 'run to Nantsillan, and inquire if Mr. Gerans has been there.'

The messenger returned to say that Mr. Gerans had been there in the morning, and had gone after Mr. Penhalligan, and that neither had returned.

After dinner the old man went out to inspect some buildings that were being repaired at the back, and to see that his cob had eaten her oats and was properly groomed.

Rose went to her room. She was restless. She looked at her face in the glass, and was shocked to see how pale she was and how red about the eyes. She soused her face well with fresh water, and, to distract her attention from her self-reproaches, changed her gown.

The room was hot, and she could not breathe. She put on her hat and went out to

walk on the down, and fill her lungs with sea-
air—and to look for Gerans.

'Where are you going?' shouted the Squire.
He was outside the calves' house, ordering a
portion of the wall to be rebuilt. 'Going to
hunt after your husband? Don't you have any
fears about him; he and Con have probably
gone fishing.'

She went on, in the direction of Nantsillan
Cove, over the track taken by Constantine that
morning. She had no intention of descending
the dangerous path. She purposed looking out
seaward, on the chance of getting a sight of
Gerans and Constantine in a boat.

Suddenly, Dennis Penhalligan stood before
her. He came abruptly on her from the steep
ascent. Rose's heart leaped and stood still
when she saw that he was alone. He did not
seem to observe her at first. His hat was
drawn over his eyes and his step was uncertain.
When he heard her call his name he looked at
her with eyes the expression of which frightened her.

'Mr. Penhalligan!' she cried, 'for pity's
sake tell me, where is my husband?'

His eyes flashed, then faded. He seemed

like a man who was recovering from a swoon,
who did not know where he was and who was
addressing him. He opened his mouth to speak,
but only an unintelligible murmur issued from
it. Rose was seriously alarmed. His manner
was enough to startle her, her conscience sufficiently aroused to warn her of danger. In her
fear she grasped his wrist, she shook him, and
said :

' Tell me, tell me, where is Gerans ? '

Then he seemed to recover himself. His
eyebrows drew together, and his eyes kindled.
He looked at her with a searching glance, and
asked in a low tone, ' Am I his keeper ? What
do I care for him ? '

Rose let go her hold. She turned deadly
pale and trembled. Her heart stood still. She
looked at him with terror, afraid to ask more.
His eyes fell. He remained before her with
his head sunk, and his nervous hand clutching
at something in his breast pocket.

' Dennis,' said Rose, ' where is he ? '

' You do not love him, why then do you
ask ? ' he said, in a hoarse whisper.

Then she laid hold of him, fiercely, frantic-
ally, with a hand on each shoulder. ' Dennis !

tell me! Have you seen him? What has happened? Where is he?'

'Let me go,' answered he, sullenly. 'Gerans will trouble you no more. He has fallen—down the rocks—into the sea—is dead!'

Then Rose uttered a scream, shriller than the cry of the sea-gulls. 'You have killed him—murderer!'

She was staggering forward to the cliff edge, unconscious whither she went, when he caught her, and said in a deep, hoarse, vibrating tone:

'Why do you cry? You did not love him.'

'I—I not love him!' She wrung her hands over her head in the air. 'O Gerans! dear husband! my dearest love! my only love! It is not true; you are not dead!'

'Rose!—you love me.'

She thrust him away with a cry of horror, and, turning, ran home, threw herself before her father-in-law on her knees, and cried: 'He is dead! He is dead! He has been murdered! O my God, have mercy on me! O my God, forgive me!'

But when she had turned from Penhalligan, with a look and cry of loathing, she heard a

laugh behind her, a laugh the like of which
she never had heard before, the sound of which
in all her after-life she never forgot. The laugh
proceeded from Dennis. He had committed
murder, and Rose loved the murdered man.
His ill fate pursued him to the last. Fate
played a hideous game with him, and mocked
him to the end. Rose loved Gerans, had loved
him all along, and had not cared for him—
Dennis. She had coquetted with him, but had
reserved for him no place in her heart. With
this torturing thought gnawing at his brain he
reached his cottage.

'Please, sir,' said little Ruth, ' will you have
some dinner? There be cold roast· beef and
pickled cauliflower.'

He started, and left the house again. He
must be alone now. He staggered up the
coombe till he came to the spot where the floor
of dead leaves lay, now as of old—the place
where Rose had bidden him not despair. He
moved like a piece of clockwork. From the
moment that he saw the white face of Gerans
before him in the Iron Gate, and fired at him,
to the moment that he met Rose on the cliffs,
he remembered nothing. He had seen Gerans,

struck by his ball, totter back, and fall from the ledge of rock into the water below, a dark pool left by the ebbed tide, which the rising tide was replenishing.

Murderer! That word uttered by Rose hammered in his ear, and would not cease. He had committed a murder. For what end? To break the heart of Rose, and to cover his soul with an indelible stain. Whether brought to justice or not mattered nothing—the self-reproach, the consciousness of guilt would never leave him, night or day.

Dead! Gerans dead! In the stupefaction that followed the first outbreak of horror, this was all that Rose could repeat. She felt every-thing spin about her. She ran into the hall, without purpose, without knowing whither she went, and fell on her knees, with her hands pressed to her brow, rocking herself in a stunned state, in which she could think of nothing. She moaned, and the tears ran over her cheeks, her brain was bursting, her heart was contracted with a spasm of pain. So old Gaverock found her. What was the meaning of her alarm? What occasion had she for her fear? Why did she frighten him without cause?

As he spoke he seemed to be turning about
the piercing sword that had penetrated to her
heart, and with every turn a fresh gash was
made. She screamed with pain.

'Rose, be rational,' said the Squire. 'Dead!
Murdered! How dead? By whom murdered?'

'He is dead; I know it,' cried Rose. 'Murdered by Dennis Penhalligan.'

'This is nonsense,' said the old man.
'Woman's exaggeration and irrational jumping
to conclusions. Why do you say this? Give
me a reason. Have you seen Gerans? How
do you know he is dead? What grounds have
you for your charge? Because he did not
return to dinner you have worked yourself into
hysterics. That is it. I know women.'

Rose somewhat recovered her senses when
thus catechised. What would she not have
given now to be able to say that she had no
grounds for believing that Dennis had killed
her husband, no grounds for supposing that he
bore him enmity! She, she herself was the
cause of the crime; her vanity, which craved
for flattery, and which was pleased with al-
luring to her such a man as Dennis. She, she
herself had murdered Gerans. She had in-

flamed the heart of Penhalligan against him.
She was as guilty of his death as if she had
murdered him with her own hand. Then there
surged up in her memory the recollection of
her unkindness to Gerans, the coldness with
which she had met his overtures, the bitterness
with which she had reproached him. ' I know
he is dead. Dennis Penhalligan told me so,'
was all she could say to her father-in-law.
Old Gaverock was angry with her tears, impatient with the difficulty of getting a statement
out of her mouth.

'I don't believe a word of it,' he said.
' Women like to imagine disasters, and enjoy
a squeal over them, knowing that there is
nothing at the bottom. I'll go to Penhalligan,
and learn from him what this means.' Then
he strode out of the house.

Rose remained where she was, a prey to
despair and self-reproach. She threw herself
in a chair, and wept and prayed, and beat her
head. The servants heard her, and peeped in
at the door, and whispered; then one of the
oldest ventured in and spoke to her, and asked
what was the matter, was she ill? She had
better have a drop of brandy.

'Go away! Leave me alone! I am not ill!' She started erect on her knees, and thrust the woman away with her right hand, with the left in her hair, which was dishevelled, and falling about her neck. She was as one mad, mad with the agony of remorse. The servant-maid withdrew; but Rose could not remain where she was, with the girls talking about her, peering in, and volunteering advice. She stood up, went out of the porch door, and tottered along the path towards Nantsillan.

Hark! a shot. She shrunk in all her muscles and nerves at the sound.

Half an hour passed. She had staggered to the garden wall, and was leaning against that, looking along the path, waiting for the return of her father-in-law. That half-hour to her went creeping along as if each minute were an hour.

Presently she saw Hender Gaverock rise from the coombe and come slowly along the way towards her. She tried to leave the wall and go to meet him, but her knees yielded under her weight. She was constrained to await him there. One look at his altered countenance sufficed to convince her that her worst fears were well founded. She had lost Gerans for ever. The face of the old Squire was grey as ashes.

'I cannot ask any questions of Dennis Penhalligan,' he said, in a low tone. 'He has shot himself through the heart.'

CHAPTER LVIII.

ON FOUR OARS.

THE old man said no more. He went past Rose, towards the house. Rose's tears dried in her eyes. She crept after her father-in-law, supporting herself against the brick garden wall till she came to the spot where Dennis had stood the evening before, watching her through the window. Vividly did she now see him, as he looked at her with his burning eyes. She cried out with fear. She fled from the spot, and stumbled over the porch steps. Dennis was dead also. Dead—by his own act. Her guilt became deeper, blacker, more hideous!

No one in Towan noticed her. There was commotion there. Old Gaverock was sending the men out to look for Gerans—or his body; and one fellow rode away towards Padstow, with loose rein, to summon the old drunken doctor, and another ran off to the farm nearest

Nantsillan, to get aid for removing the body of Penhalligan from the glade to his house.

Rose crouched on the steps, holding to a granite ball that ornamented the low wall that enclosed them. Her shame was more than she could bear. For some time she could not cry, but at last the tears began to flow again, and as they flowed they washed away all the false colours with which she had disguised to herself the relations in which she had stood to Dennis, colours painted on with the hand of discontent, vanity, and weakness. She knew her guilt. She could no longer excuse her conduct, and the breath of death blew away all the ashes which had overlain and threatened to choke the glowing embers of her real love for Gerans.

Hitherto Rose had lived in a dream of pleasure and self-confidence. Now she was rudely awakened to see the ruin that her thoughtlessness had brought on herself and others.

Squire Gaverock went out with his men, and searched the shore of Sandymouth and Nantsillan Cove in vain. They ran out the boats and explored the rocks where they rose

out of the sea. They could find no trace of
the presence of Gerans, alive or dead. After a
search of some hours the Squire came home.
He bade his men continue their examination of
the coast ; he returned to inquire if any tidings
of his lost son had reached Towan during his
absence. He found that none had.

Then he entered his study, and threw himself into his chair, to consider what was to be
done. He passed his hand over his eyes and
brow, and the hand shook as he did so. However often he made this movement he was
unable to brush away the picture of Dennis
lying on the mat of russet autumn leaves,
cemented together with the rain and rot of
winter, with a pistol falling from his lifeless
hand, and the blood clotted on his breast over
the heart.

Would Penhalligan have destroyed himself
had Rose's accusation been unfounded ? This
question insisted on being answered, but he
strove to put the question away from him.
Why had Rose accused him ? Was it only
because Dennis had informed her of the death
of her husband, or did some dreadful mystery
lurk behind this into which he dare not look ?

The old man's mouth quivered, as did his hand. One dark mystery after another stole through his thoughts, unexplained, which he feared to attempt to solve. A tide was rising and surrounding him, and each wave that leaped higher was more threatening than the last. What lay before him? What were the discoveries that would be forced on him? He heard Rose's foot in the hall. He would not go out to her. He would not speak to her. He shrank from even looking at her. To what extent was she responsible for what had taken place? He dared not ask her, or ask himself.

The ambition of his life was at an end. In one moment his pride, his desire, were broken down. His hopes, his ambitions, had been centred in his son, and lay dead with him.

Suddenly he started back in his chair, and ran it against the bookcase, and sat staring at the drawer of his table. The drawer had been tampered with. There were marks on it that an effort had been made to open it, and that the lock had been broken. He stood up and put his hand to the drawer. It opened readily. The lock was torn off, the mahogany bruised. The money was gone. Purse and pocket-book—

the purse with the gold, the pocket-book with the notes—all were gone.

Who was the robber? Had this robbery any connection with the loss of Gerans and the self-destruction of Penhalligan? The number of questions rising before the old man's mind and demanding replies was growing and becoming bewildering. He was led from darkness to deeper darkness, into night profound.

His mind went at once to Constantine. That Gerans had taken the money did not suggest itself to him. That Dennis had done so, been caught in the act by Gerans, that Dennis had killed him to conceal his theft, and then, finding he could not escape, had shot himself, was a possible solution. But then, where was Constantine? Why was he away? Why had not signs of him been seen? The brothers had not gone out boating together. Every boat that belonged to Towan was in its place. Where was Constantine to give them some information about Gerans? Then, suddenly, it occurred to the old man that if Penhalligan had taken the money, the purse and note-book would be found on him. He ought to have remained by the corpse and examined the pockets. But he

had been too alarmed and anxious to find
Gerans to consider that ; besides, when Dennis
was discovered, the Squire had no suspicion
that the money was taken.

Where was Constantine ? Constantine had
wanted the money. He was impatient to have
it at once ; he had refused to stay more than a
day. There was a mystery about Constantine.
He had darkly hinted that he was in danger of
arrest for some crime. The Squire had put
this from him as an attempt to extort the money
from him by playing on his family pride. But
now he began to fear that there was some
truth in the threat. Constantine had taken
money elsewhere, or forged a name. That
would explain both his reticence and his eagerness to get away. He had not told his parents
that he was alive because he wished it to be
thought generally that he was dead, and that
so his guilt might not be disclosed. By some
means it had been found out that he was not
dead, and he had come home to be helped to
escape from the country, and now that this
help had been delayed he had taken the money
from his father's drawer, and gone. Perhaps
this was the story of Constantine, the old man

thought, with a flush on his brow, and with clenched hands.

But—what had this to do with the disappearance of Gerans and the suicide of Dennis? Time alone could solve these riddles. Then a fresh horror came on him, and made him gasp. If Gerans were dead, then his estate, and the representation of the family, the headship of the Gaverocks—*Toujours sans tache*—would devolve on Constantine, on this runagate, this wretch who robbed his own father and wife, who was flying from justice! What would become of Towan in the hands of an unprincipled scoundrel, who dare not show his face in England? He groaned. He would have paid out his heart's blood to the last drop cheerfully at that moment, if with it he could redeem Gerans from death. He compared the two brothers, so strangely alike in face and build; and now a flame of real love flashed up through the thick crust of pride that he had suffered to grow over his heart. Gerans had always been an obedient, amiable son, had never given him annoyance, had been ever upright and true and manly.

He had not treated Gerans properly; he

had exacted from him submission with despotic authority, he had not considered his years, and that he ought to have taken him into counsel, and listened to his opinion. He saw by the unselfishness of Gerans, with which he had stood forth on behalf of his brother, that his heart was good to the core ; he saw by the pertinacity with which he held to his determination, that he was bold where he felt he was right. A feeling of pride at the recognition of the merits of Gerans woke up in the old man's soul, and now the tears began to trickle down his cheeks, from eyes that had not been thus moistened since childhood.

Alas ! no tears, no love, no recognition, would bring back the dead.

Squire Gaverock went to Nantsillan. He put on his roughest manner to disguise his emotion. He found the house overrun with the curious ; no one was in authority, every one had as much right there as another. He drove them all out except the farmer's wife, Mrs. Jemima Josse, and the charwoman, and old Mary Tregothnan, who undertook to lay the body out ; all the gentlefolks liked her to lay them out, she explained, she did make such pretty

corpses of them. Then he inquired whether
any money had been found in the pockets of
the dead man, any purse, any note-books. Yes,
a leather purse had been found that contained
a few shillings. Farmer Josse had taken charge
of that as he was constable. Yes, there had
been discovered one note-book; it was pro-
duced, and the Squire saw it was the surgeon's
pocket register of his visits and the maladies of
the patients visited. Mr. Gaverock made strict
inquiries, and had no occasion to doubt that
this was all. The constable, Mr. Josse, had
been on the spot when the body was moved,
and had seen and taken note of everything the
pockets contained. The Squire placed Mrs.
Josse in charge. She was an old servant of
Towan, her husband a tenant; Nantsillan was
the property of the Gaverocks, and Squire
Hender was Justice of Peace. He was accordingly obeyed promptly.

Then he returned to Towan. As his face
was directed homeward the stern and rough
expression deserted it, and it became haggard
and distressed.

' Any news ? ' he asked.

There was none.

'Where is Mrs. Rose?'

'Please your honour, her's upstairs, a-locked into the bedroom, a-crying like blazes. Us have took her up some tea and toast, but her won't touch it.'

'Go, someone, upstairs, and tell her to come to me into the study. Tell her I insist on her obedience.'

He went into the library and cast himself into the chair.

In a few moments Rose entered, so changed in face and manner that the Squire looked at her some time with surprise without speaking.

'Rose,' said he at last, 'are you now sufficiently composed to answer questions in a rational manner?'

She looked up at him. He thought her eyes filled her face, so large were they, so shrunk were her fresh and rounded cheeks. Her lips moved, but she could not speak. The lips had lost their cherry redness.

'Rose,' he said, 'tell me everything you know, everything that can help me to understand what has happened. There is something behind this to which I cannot get, and which you, perhaps, may disclose.'

'I will tell you everything,' she answered slowly, then paused to gather up her courage and strength for the avowal.

In that pause she and the old man heard a step on the hall floor that they knew, and held their breath.

The study door opened, and he whom they believed to be dead came in.

Squire Gaverock grasped the arms of his chair, and half rose from it. That was Gerans, certainly, before him, and not his ghost, though Gerans looked pale and dejected. Rose uttered a cry, flew to his breast, and threw her arms round him.

'Gerans! Gerans! you are alive!'

Her cry was as full of joy and ecstasy of love as the song that breaks from the throat of a nightingale on a still spring night. It went direct to the heart of Gerans, who understood its meaning, and he put his arm round her, and held her to his beating heart, whilst with the other hand he pressed back the white brow that was buried in his bosom, in order that he might look into her eyes. She dared not yet meet his steady, inquiring eyes, and she shook her head from his hold, and laid it on his shoulder, and burst into a storm of tears.

Old Squire Gaverock held out his hand. 'So, so—a false alarm. That is well.' He drew a long breath. 'Women are fools. With my sixty-five years, Golly! I ought to have known better than believe their alarms. Gerans, we thought you were dead.'

'I am alive and sound,' answered Gerans, with astonishment. 'This is not the first time I have absented myself from dinner.'

'Where is Constantine?'

'Is he not here? I have not seen him.'

'Gerans, where did you part from Penhalligan?'

'At the waterfall into the cove.'

'What had you to do with him?' asked the Squire, gravely.

'With Dennis? Oh, we had a conversation.'

'And an altercation?'

'Not on my side. I apologised to him for our conduct to Loveday. I shall speak about that presently.'

'Do you not know what has happened?'

'Happened?—to him?—no. I parted from him many hours ago.'

'Rose charged him with having murdered you, and he has shot himself.'

Gerans stared at his father with horror and perplexity. He became pale as death, whilst Rose clung to him more passionately. He put his hand over his eyes, and tried to collect his thoughts.

'I do not understand this,' he said. 'Dennis has been for some time incensed against us, against me for not taking up Loveday's cause with the vigour that I ought to have shown, and for something else I need not mention.' He felt Rose's arms contract convulsively about him, and heard a sob escape her labouring bosom. 'And he has been irritated with you, father, for sending Loveday away and not acknowledging her, as you ought to have done. Then ensued the disappearance of Loveday. It is possible that poor Dennis's mind has become disturbed. I did not think him himself when I left him this morning. I did not tell him plainly that Constantine had returned. I do not think he had heard of it, or he would have mentioned it to me. I only told him that a great surprise and joy were in store for Loveday.'

'Gerans,' said Rose, looking up in his face,

through her tears, 'dear Gerans, he told me that you were dead. He had seen you fall.'

'His mind was disturbed,' said Gerans, 'poor fellow! My God! what troubles, what sorrows come on us!'

Neither his father nor his wife had anything to say to this. A tear came from Gerans's eye and fell on the cheek of Rose, a tear of sorrow for his friend.

Then they heard a tramp of feet, and, looking through the study window, they saw eight men approach the house carrying four oars crossed on their shoulders, and on the oars lay a body.

Before the eight men walked another, carrying a bundle.

'They are bringing him here!' cried Rose, cowering into her husband's breast in terror. 'Oh, do not let them! Why should they bring him here?—this is not his home. Let him be taken to Nantsillan.'

Gerans disengaged himself from her clinging arms. He looked steadily through the window, then he turned quickly back, and said : 'Stay, stay here, Rose. Do not leave the room. Father, this is not Dennis. Prepare your mind for another and worse disaster.' He had recognised his red-topped boots on the legs of the man who was being borne by the eight. He knew that Constantine had put them on that morning.

The old Squire stood up, trembling like an aspen, with white face.

' God be gracious to us ! ' he gasped. ' Give me your arm, Gerans. I—I find my feet fail me. Not—it is not—Constantine ? '

In another moment the tramp of the feet was in the hall. Then with a sigh of relief the eight bearers put down their burden upon the long oak dinner table, withdrew the oars and wiped their brows with their sleeves.

The ninth man placed the bundle at the foot of the dead man who lay on the gate—a man in a suit of Gerans's clothes, with his fine frilled shirt, and with his red-topped boots ; and with his white face streaked with blood from a wound in the forehead where a bullet had pierced his brain. In death, Constantine bore a strange and striking likeness to his brother, who now stood nearly as white, and with as rigid a face, bending over him.

' Here, your honour,' said the man who

had carried the bundle, 'here be two pocket-books and a purse us have took out of his coat pockets, lest they should fall and be lost. I reckon they be chuck full of money. And us be dry, and would like a drop of cider.'

CHAPTER LIX.

RECONCILIATION.

THAT evening when Gerans came to his room for the night he found Rose, dressed as she had been, sitting on the sofa awaiting him. He was late, he had sat up long in conversation with his father. He was surprised to find Rose not gone to bed.

'Oh, Rose,' he said, with a little reproach in his tone, 'you will overtire yourself. You should be asleep at this hour.'

'No, Gerans, no,' she replied. 'I could not sleep till I had spoken with you. Tell me, tell me all. You think that Dennis shot Constantine, and then went away and destroyed himself. Why did he kill Constantine?'

'He bore him a grudge. Con had behaved very badly towards Loveday. Con had first married her secretly, and made her promise not to tell what had been done, but to leave to him the communication to his parents. He took advantage of her promise, and did not tell any one. Then, when it came out, he hid himself somewhere —where, perhaps, we shall never learn—and allowed Loveday to suppose he was dead. That was cruel and unjust treatment, and no doubt Dennis felt it keenly ; he was a man of strong passions, and resented it. I had been speaking to him in the morning on the matter, but I could make nothing out of him. I suppose he was wild with rage because he had heard that Constantine was alive and home again. He left his house armed with a pistol. He went to find Con, and ask him his intentions, to know what he meant to do about Loveday. What ensued when they met no one now can tell, but I conjecture that there was a quarrel ; Constantine did not satisfy Dennis, and Dennis, blind with anger, shot him. Then he woke to the full horror of what he had done, and destroyed himself.'

'That is the way in which you explain the whole story?' asked Rose, looking him questio ingly in the eyes. 'That you think accounts for everything?'

'It explains all,' he answered, but with some hesitation.

'Gerans,' said Rose, with a firmness unusual in her, 'Gerans, dear husband, no—it was not so.'

'Rose!' he exclaimed, and shuddered. 'Rose! enough. It is explained.'

'No, Gerans, no. This will not do. You shall know the whole truth. I will not hide anything from you. No, Gerans, it was not so at all—Dennis Penhalligan shot Constantine because he mistook him for you.'

'Rose! Rose!'

'I have more to say. I am guilty, I, even I, of the death of Constantine and of Dennis. It was I, by my vanity and love of admiration, who lured Dennis on, till he was mad with love for me and hate for you. But, oh, Gerans, I swear to you, by the God who stands above the starry sky, that I have not loved any but you.'

'I will believe you,' he said, sadly. 'I have always trusted you. I have loved you—in spite of all.'

'In spite of my folly, my temper, my wicked words!' she said, and her tears began to flow. 'Oh, Gerans! I know now how wicked I have been. Here, in this very room, I treated you cruelly, when you returned with inflamed eyes from St. Ives. You asked me to stay with you, and I would not. I wanted to be away with the company below.' She threw herself on her knees before him. 'I am unworthy of you, Gerans; indeed, indeed, I am.'

He tried to raise her. 'Say no more, Rose. Your acknowledgment of having done wrong is the utmost you can do to efface the past.'

'I will not rise,' she said, 'till you know everything. I will tell you all, I will tell you what the thoughts of my heart were, as well as the words I said. I will not be forgiven till you know the truth as clearly as I can put it.'

'Rose, I also have to ask your pardon. I was too yielding to my father.'

'No, Gerans, you were right, and I was wrong. You did not oppose your father, because my whims were unreasonable. You were right not to let me have my own way. Because I have taken my course it has led me to this.'

He raised her from the floor, and made her

sit by his side on the sofa; and there he, with
his arm round her, and her wet face in his
breast, listened to the whole story of her
frivolity, her play with Dennis—to his coming
and standing outside the window on the previous evening. She told him of the ride to
church on Phœbus, of everything that had
passed on that expedition, of her brief repentance in church, and the return of her bad
spirit on the way home; she told him of her
foolish jealousy of Loveday; she told him of
the kiss Dennis had given her at the well.
She hid nothing from him. 'But, oh, Gerans, I
never, never, loved any one but you, and I
wanted to make you love me more by forcing
you to become jealous.'

'But I was not jealous.'

'No—because you could not believe me as
bad as I was.' He drew her close to his heart,
and the bond between them was resealed, to
last unstrained, unbroken, till death.

.   .   .   .   .

The brothers-in-law were buried the same
day, and at the same time. Indeed, the two
coffins were borne to the church in one pro-
cession—first that of Constantine, then that of

Penhalligan ; and one body of mourners attended both—first walked Squire Gaverock with Loveday on his arm, then Gerans with Madam Loveys, then Mr. Loveys and Rose, and finally Anthony, junior.

The news of the deaths of Dennis and of Constantine Gaverock had spread through the country. It was in the papers. Thus Loveday had been apprised of her brother's and husband's simultaneous decease. She sent at once to Marsland for Paul Featherstone. When he came to the cottage, she told him everything. The necessity for keeping silence was removed.

One request she made, that Juliot might never be told of her husband's treachery. Let her know that he was dead—not that he had led her into a dishonourable marriage, which cast a stain on her child.

Paul was too astonished at the revelation to be able to determine at once what should be done.

'I must return immediately to Nantsillan,' said Loveday, earnestly, entreatingly, to Mr. Featherstone. 'I must attend the funeral of my brother ; and I will go, if need be, on my knees to Mr. Gaverock to beseech him to keep the secret of my marriage. It need never be known now.'

Nothing had come out at the double inquest. One man had been found shot through the head, the other through the heart, both killed by the same weapon, a double-barrelled pistol. Dennis was found in the wood, lying dead on the dry leaves ; Constantine was washed ashore by the tide in the cove. It was not till long after that the boat in the Iron Gate was discovered. The tide had carried his body out of Porth-Ierne, and cast it up below the waterfall.

No motive could be attributed to Dennis for killing him. No one but the Gaverocks knew of the marriage. Little Ruth was called, to account for Penhalligan going out with the pistol. She was able most confidently to assert that Mr. Constantine had not been to the cottage, and that Mr. Dennis had complained of annoyance from a dog that haunted him. Who had seen the dog? No one else. The supposition arrived at was that Mr. Penhalligan was suffering from disturbance of the brain, that accidentally he had shot Mr. Constantine Gaverock, and that then, horror struck at what he had done, he had destroyed himself.

The verdict on Constantine was ' Accidental
death ' ; that on Dennis was ' Suicide whilst in
a state of unsound mind.' Neither Rose nor
Gerans was called to give evidence. Properly,
Rose ought to have been summoned, as she had
given the first notice of a tragedy, but she was
spared the painfulness of so doing. The old
Squire deposed to the finding of the body of
Dennis ; no evidence appeared necessitating
the call of Gerans. That was well, for he could
not have kept back the subject of conversation
with Dennis if closely interrogated. The real
cause of the murder and suicide was never
known to Loveday or to the Squire ; two only
knew it, and they kept it locked in their own
breasts.

Madam Loveys with her son and husband
would not return to Towan after the funeral.
The lady had ordered a carriage to await them in
the village to carry them home. She made her
son mount the box, and put her husband inside,
and then, when they were seated, entered the
carriage herself, and ordered the coachman to
drive on. As soon as old Gaverock with Loveday, Gerans and Rose, and the servant had returned to Towan, the Squire called his son and

daughters-in-law into the library, and bade them be seated.

The old man was greatly altered—his hair was greyer and less rough, his eyes had lost their commanding flash, his complexion was less hale, his hand less steady, his gait less confident, his voice was lower, and his manner had ceased to be boisterous.

'Is the door shut behind you, Gerans?'

'Yes, father.'

'My children,' said the Squire, and his eyes as he said 'my children' rested on Loveday as well as Rose, 'we have now a single duty to perform, a duty that has been delayed too long Our Loveday must have right done her. She must receive immediate acknow-ledgment. I blame myself for having denied it to her so long. Now it shall be accorded to her fully and publicly. This house is hence-forth her home, our name is her name, we form but one family, and I am her father as truly as I am yours, Rose. From me she can count on receiving henceforth deference and love.'

'Yes,' said Gerans, 'so it must be.'

Then, Loveday, who was pale as snow but

composed, said, 'No, dear Mr. Gaverock. If
I have any claims upon you, let me claim your
submission to one thing I ask. Let the past
be forgotten. Do not let it be known that I
married Constantine.'

'Not—why not?'

'For his sake,' she answered. 'We must
think of the dead, and spare his memory. I may
say for my poor brother's sake also; I would
have his memory also spared. If it transpire
that I was married to Constantine privately,
and that he did not let his marriage be known,
people will at once suspect that the death of
Constantine was not accidental, that Dennis
shot him out of revenge for the wrong he conceived that he had done to his sister. I do
not myself believe this—but that is what people
will say.'

The old man considered. This was certainly
true.

'Did Constantine not communicate with you
after he disappeared and we believed him dead?'
asked Gerans.

'No,' replied Loveday. 'I received no letter, no tidings of any sort from him. Till quite
recently I, like you, believed him to be dead.'

'I suppose we shall never know where he was during the time between when he was washed off the keel of the "Mermaid" and when he reappeared the other day here to meet, as it proved, his death.'

The old man said this musingly, and Loveday did not contradict him. He never did learn where Constantine had been, for Loveday never told. She held back this from the Squire lest she should add to *his* shame and sorrow, and he held back from her the truth about Constantine breaking open his drawer and stealing her money lest he should add to *her* sorrow.

'I do not ask of you to publish what for my sake, for the sake of Constantine, and for the sake of Dennis, had better be kept secret,' said Loveday; 'let all that miserable story be buried from the world, and forgotten, if possible, by ourselves.'

'Come by me, Loveday,' said the old man, gently. When she obeyed, he drew her hand within his, and stroked it with his rough but unnerved hand.

'My Loveday, my dear, very dear Loveday,' he said, 'I am sixty-five years old, and I thought I knew women, but I am only be-

ginning to know them now. Loveday, I did
think it was conferring a great honour on you
to allow you to bear our name, but I am not
so sure of that now.' He leaned his elbow on
the table, and thrust his left hand through his
grey hair, whilst clear tears rolled down his
cheeks. 'Dishonour has been brought on the
name of Gaverock by—by my son, and perhaps
you do well to refuse to bear it. Aye, though
you may not know all, it is so—dishonour.'

Loveday rose and put her arms round his
neck, whilst the tears welled out of her eyes.

'No, dear Mr. Gaverock, do not say that.
It is because I love and respect that name that
I would ward off from it the breath of reproach.'
Then she kissed him.

He still held her hand. 'But you will stay
with us here, you will make this a home? I
will not be domineering or violent any more.
Gerans, I have to ask your forgiveness. Here,
before your wife, I must acknowledge that you
are sometimes right, and that I esteem you for
holding your ground when your conscience for-
bids a surrender. Rose, I must ask your forgiveness also. I have tried you also. I have

been to blame. My poor wife, I wish she were here, I would ask her forgiveness also. I did not understand her. By the way, Gerans, have you an old hat that will fit me? I won't go about bareheaded any more—by Golly! I won't.'

CHAPTER LX.

A BED OF VIOLETS.

A TWELVEMONTH—nay, more—had passed, winter had set in and tossed its foam over the cliffs, and the wind had carried the roar of the wintry Atlantic far inland. Spring, summer, autumn passed, and now as the last leaves were shed in Nantsillan glen, Loveday was stooping over her old bed of purple violets, picking a bunch. She had a little basket on her left arm, slung on the wrist; she wore long black mittens from her elbows to her hands. She had no bonnet on, but a shawl was thrown over her head and pinned under her chin. The fern in the coombe was as brown as copper, but the moss in revenge was showing itself vividly green. Here and there the blue bugloss, and with it pink cranesbill, remained in flower, defying the wintry winds, smiling under a clouded sky. A few rooks were cawing, and jackdaws chattering; a

yellow finch swinging on a maple twig was
piping. No bird was disturbed by Loveday.
She stooped and passed her fingers among the
green leaves, and plucked each violet that was
discovered, and made them into a little cluster.
Some were in the basket; she put her bunches
into the basket, not the several violets as picked.
The shawl over her head was much the same in
colour as the flowers she gathered. Her gown
was black, with a white lace fringe about the
sleeves and flounce.

She was so engrossed in gathering violets
that she did not hear the fall of a step behind
her.

'How do you do, Miss—Mrs. I mean—Loveday?'

She started, rose upright, turned, and the
colour came into her cheeks and a light into
her dark eyes.

'Oh, Mr. Featherstone, I am so heartily glad
to see you!'

'Excuse me,' he said, 'I apologise for calling
you by your Christian name, but I was hardly
able to decide by what name to address you
with strict truth and to avoid giving pain.' He
was the same stiff, pragmatical man, haggling

about trifles, yet sincere to his heart's core. She held out her hand to him, after passing the violets from the right hand to the left.

He bowed over it, and with old-fashioned courtesy, old-fashioned even then, pressed his lips to her fingers.

'Your hand is fragrant with violets,' he said, 'and what marvel, when you are as a violet yourself, sweet, and hiding beneath the leaves.'

'Pardon me, sir,' said Loveday, 'I am standing on the leaves; look above me, all are fallen.'

'I was speaking metaphorically,' said Paul, with a slight tone of vexation, but so slight that it was lost as soon as perceived. 'I have ventured to search for you, madam, as I doubted how to ask after you at the door of Towan. Should I inquire for Miss Penhalligan, or for Mrs. Rock—pardon me, Mrs. Gaverock, I mean. I was unaware to what extent circumstances were known, and under which name you were now pleased to pass. So I wandered and waited about till I lighted upon you, and now, most appropriately, I find you at a violet bed. You will take no offence, madam, if I say that in my mind the violet is so associated with your sweet self that at Marsland my sister Juliot, who shares

my views in everything, and myself always regard the violet bed under the wall as sacred to
the memory of one whom we have both learned
to love and revere.'

Loveday would have been puzzled by his
odd address had she not known the man, and
been able to allow for his formal ways. She
was really pleased to see him, she had the
warmest regard for him, she valued him as a
man perfectly true, sincere, upright; she smiled
at his quaint ways and rather liked them, they
savoured of old-world manners, and there was
a lack of these in Towan which made her ready
to condone some exaggeration in Paul Featherstone.

'How is Juliot?' she asked. 'I have longed
to hear, yet did not like to write.'

'Juliot is well, and the little Con is also well
and very flourishing,' answered Paul Featherstone. 'There will be a Stanbury of Stanbury
yet. I have spent forty pounds in obtaining a
royal licence for young Master Con to assume
the name of Stanbury in place of Rock, so that
henceforth that little urchin is Squire Stanbury
of Stanbury, and our dear mother's name will
flourish anew in him.'

'What—what does Juliot know?' asked Loveday, timidly.

'Nothing. I have stood as a wall about her, fencing her from the knowledge, and now all danger is past. She still believes in a Mr. Rock, and supposes he has been drowned. Her great grief is that his body has not been recovered. I would not for anything in this world that she should be undeceived. Juliot is a child in heart, and has the faith of a child. Were she to learn what a wicked—excuse me—were she to know all, her faith in the goodness of mankind would receive such a shock that the childlike spirit in her would droop and die. No—she shall never know—never, so help me, God!' He took off his hat at the last words. Then he covered again and continued, 'And I—I also must ask, what is known here?'

'Nothing,' answered Loveday. 'That is to say, only Mr. Gaverock and Gerans know the truth, and it is their wish now, as well as mine, that the past should be buried.'

'So the marriage of Constantine Gaverock and Loveday Penhalligan is to remain hidden in the parish register of the church in Exeter where you were married?'

'Yes. It is so, indeed.'

'Then,' said Paul, 'should you ever be married again it seems to me that the most suitable proceeding would be for you to be re-married in that same church, that the two registers might be preserved in the same book, so no disguise or evasion of the truth would be needed, and such disguise or evasion would be very painful, and hardly to be justified.'

Loveday coloured, then laughed, and said: 'We need not consider remote eventualities, Mr. Featherstone. We will talk of Juliot and little Con. Is he much grown? Is he a dear pet? How many teeth has he? What colour is his hair—and his eyes?'

'Pardon me, at this moment I cannot talk of little Con. He is a dear little daisyflower. But who thinks of the daisy when he lights on the violet? Nor is that such a remote contingency as you consider, that is if you would deign—that is to say—if your humble servant should find favour in your eyes.'

The bunch of violets fell from Loveday's hand, and the colour deserted her cheeks.

'I am well aware,' continued Paul; he removed his hat and, kneeling stiffly, began to pick up the violets that she had let fall. 'I am well aware,' he said whilst thus engaged, 'that I am unworthy to solicit such a treasure. I have sinned against you most deeply, and should not dare to appear before you now were I not convinced that in you every sweetness and beauty of soul were to be found, the quality of mercy, the grace of generosity included. I had the mad folly at one time to doubt you. Now, reviewing the past, I am covered with shame at the thought that I should have been so wicked, so graceless, as to doubt *you*. You—you are to me the ideal of womanhood, all gentleness, truth, self-surrender, pity. I do not ask you if you have cared for me. I know that when you were under my roof you suffered the bitterest of pains. I know that then into the pure temple of your soul no thought of me could enter, dedicated then as it was to another, though that other was unworthy. I ask only to make some amends to you for the wrong I did in mistrusting you, and I ask for Juliot's sake. She wants a sister to guide, comfort, and help her. I know my own unworthiness, but I know also that as you have seen Juliot you must love her. So—take me for my sister's sake.'

Loveday was trembling. She knew the man at her feet, his perfect integrity, his chivalrous honour and love of truth; she was not blind to his weaknesses.

'Madam!' he said, 'I have picked up all the violets. I do not ask you to speak. What shall I do with the violets? Am I to take the little posy and carry it away with me as the only remembrance I have of the one woman whom I love and regard above every other woman under heaven? Or may I put the violets into your basket, and help you to carry the sweet and pretty burden?'

She hesitated but for a moment, and then held out the little basket to him.

The air about them was fragrant with violets.

.   .   .   .   .   .

The bells of Wellcombe were ringing a peal in the fresh summer air a twelvemonth after the events last recorded. The wind carried their music in waves inland, much as wave on wave flows with the tide upon the shore. At the entrance of the avenue to Marsland is an arch of laurel and fir and flowers.

Many people are gathered in the avenue, more outside, lining the pretty lane past the

spring, up the hill, away towards the Stratton
road. All are in their Sunday clothes; the
children have bunches of flowers in their hands.

Hark!

The cracking of postillions' whips are heard,
and down the hill amidst cheers comes a carriage, the horses and the boys with white favours.
The cheers swell into a roar of applause. At
the entrance to the avenue the carriage draws
up, and a servant lets down the steps. Then
Paul Featherstone descends, and holds out his
hand for a lady.

At the same moment from the gateway
appears Juliot in black, with a widow's cap, and
a baby on her left arm, running forward to put
her disengaged arm round the lady, and laugh
and cry together for joy of heart.

'Welcome! welcome! darling Loveday!'

Then the bride, who is in a soft grey silk,
with white bonnet, veil, and orange flowers, with
a face almost as white as the orange blossoms,
but with her large dark eyes alight with pleasure and gratitude, bows to the tenants and
cottagers who crowd round to touch and take
her hand, and the children to thrust their posies
on her.

'I think,' said Paul, 'that we shall have to change the name of this place from Mars-land to the Land of Venus, for no wars will be fought here in this home of love. This, Juliot, you will perceive, is a sort of a joke!'

'Oh, Paul! how glad I am to hear you joking again! You are so humorous.'

.   .   .   .   .   .

'Good heavens, Loveday! how came you by that?' asked Paul one day, when all his wife's effects were being unpacked and arranged in her room and drawers. The china vases, relics of her mother, had been placed on the mantelshelf. The sampler had been hung in the hall. The piano had been put in the drawing-room. Paul pointed to none of these things, but to a small double-barrelled pistol.

Loveday shuddered. 'Oh, Paul! I do not know how that has come among my goods. It —it——' She did not finish her sentence.

He was turning and examining it.

'Loveday, this is very singular. Do you see this little silver shield let in, with our arms on it—a chevron between three ostrich plumes, and above it P. F., my uncle's initials as well as mine. The pistol has never been mine; it must

have belonged to him. How did you come by
it?'

'Oh, Paul, dear Paul, throw it into the sea!
Do not let it remain with us. I did not know
it was in my box. That was the weapon which
robbed poor Constantine and Dennis of their
lives.'

Mr. Featherstone put the weapon down, as
if it burnt his fingers, but he still looked at it
with a puzzled face.

'But, Loveday, how did Dennis come by
it?'

Just then, with a shiver, Loveday thought
of the red-waistcoated pedlar, and then of the
picture in the hall of the old rover Featherstone.

'Paul,' she said, 'I cannot tell you now.
I will some day; but it seems to me as though
the spirit of your uncle could not rest till it had
wrought out its revenge on the family of Gaverock, and taken blood for blood. We will
speak about it another time.'

.   .   .   .   .   .

'Juliot!' said Paul one day, on coming home
to Marsland from a ride to Stanbury, whither
he had been summoned, 'the storms have been
ripping the roof again at the little Squire's place.

We must make it snug for him, but it will cost money.'

'Oh, please,' said Loveday, raising her dark pleading eyes, 'if you want slates, would you mind ordering them from Captain Quance, of the Towan quarries. I have a specimen slab in my bedroom, which I brought with me when I first came here. He—he almost forced me to take it; he was very kind.'

'Certainly. I will send a boat thither for a load. But pray, Loveday, what are you going to do with that red flannel?'

'I am going to send it home by my little maid Ruth, before Christmas, to an old woman, Mary Tregothnan, who suffers from rheumatism. And—dear Paul—you have lost Willy Penrose. Would you mind taking on Ruth's brother as stable boy? He once got for me two addled gull's eggs, which was very thoughtful of him, and I do not like to seem ungrateful.'

'To be sure I will,' answered Paul. 'Love-day, you have only to ask me for anything and you shall have it; to express a wish, and it shall be fulfilled. Since you have been here the whole house has been sweet with your presence, as with the fragrance of violets, that bloom and are sweet throughout the year. I *love* the *day* that brought you here, and made Loveday mine own. Heaven has made my day of life a day of love. Which,' he added after a pause, 'though it sounds like a joke, is not a joke, but a plain statement of fact.'

THE END.